PENGUIN BOOKS

STRANGERS

'Brookner writes beautifully, compelling and rewarding' *Scotsman*

'Beautifully rendered' *Observer*

'Excellent. Brookner writes beautifully' *Metro*

'Quietly brilliant' *Red*

'Poignant, fearless' *She*

'Cunningly captivating' *Good Housekeeping*

'A marvellously atmospheric meditation on loneliness' *Vogue*

'Elegant, heartfelt. Soon casts a spell on the reader' *Tatler*

'Brookner's as ferociously determined to present us with the harsh facts of life as Philip Roth or Michel Houellebecq. *Strangers* is nothing less than a great horror story' *Evening Standard*

'Consistently absorbing, uplifting' *Daily Telegraph*

'This elegant, wistful novel confronts our ultimate fears' *Mail on Sunday*

ABOUT THE AUTHOR

Anita Brookner was born in London in 1928 and, apart from several years in Paris, has lived there ever since. She trained as an art historian and taught at the Courtauld Institute of Art until 1988. *Strangers* is her twenty-fourth novel.

Strangers

ANITA BROOKNER

PENGUIN BOOKS

PENGUIN BOOKS

Published by the Penguin Group
Penguin Books Ltd, 80 Strand, London WC2R 0RL, England
Penguin Group (USA), Inc., 375 Hudson Street, New York, New York 10014, USA
Penguin Group (Canada), 90 Eglinton Avenue East, Suite 700, Toronto, Ontario, Canada M4P 2Y3
(a division of Pearson Penguin Canada Inc.)
Penguin Ireland, 25 St Stephen's Green, Dublin 2, Ireland (a division of Penguin Books Ltd)
Penguin Group (Australia), 250 Camberwell Road, Camberwell, Victoria 3124, Australia
(a division of Pearson Australia Group Pty Ltd)
Penguin Books India Pvt Ltd, 11 Community Centre, Panchsheel Park, New Delhi – 110 017, India
Penguin Group (NZ), 67 Apollo Drive, Rosedale, North Shore 0632, New Zealand
(a division of Pearson New Zealand Ltd)
Penguin Books (South Africa) (Pty) Ltd, 24 Sturdee Avenue, Rosebank, Johannesburg 2196, South Africa

Penguin Books Ltd, Registered Offices: 80 Strand, London WC2R 0RL, England

www.penguin.com

First published by Fig Tree 2009
Published in Penguin Books 2010

1

Copyright © Anita Brookner, 2009

The moral right of the author has been asserted

Printed in Great Britain by Clays Ltd, St Ives plc

A CIP catalogue record for this book is available from the British Library

ISBN: 978-0-141-04026-4

www.greenpenguin.co.uk

Penguin Books is committed to a sustainable future
for our business, our readers and our planet.
The book in your hands is made from paper
certified by the Forest Stewardship Council.

'For all its glory England is a land for rich and healthy people.
Also they should not be too old.'

Sigmund Freud, London, 1938

Author's Note

All the characters in this novel are imaginary. But I do not doubt that somewhere, out there, they, or others like them, exist.

I

Sturgis had always known that it was his destiny to die among strangers. The childhood he remembered so dolefully had been darkened by fears which maturity had done nothing to alleviate. Now, in old age, his task was to arrange matters in as seemly a manner as possible in order to spare the feelings of those strangers whose pleasant faces he encountered every morning – in the supermarket, on the bus – and whom, even now, he was anxious not to offend.

He lived alone, in a flat which had once represented the pinnacle of attainment but which now depressed him beyond measure. Hence the urge to get out into the street, among those strangers who were in a way his familiars, but not, but never, his intimates. He exchanged pleasantries with these people, but had learned, painfully, never to stray outside certain limits. The weather was a safe topic: he listened carefully to weather forecasts in order to prepare himself for a greeting of sorts should the occasion arise, while recognizing the absurd anxiety that lay behind such preparations, and perhaps aware that his very assiduity counted against him, arousing irritation, even suspicion. But codes of conduct that had applied in his youth were now obsolete. Politeness was misconstrued these days, but in any event he had never learned to accommodate indifference. Indifference if anything made him more gallant, more courteous, and the offence was thus compounded. And these were the people he relied upon to see him out of this world! Exasperation might save him, though that too must be discreetly veiled, indulged only in private. Hence the problem of finding fault with those whose job it would be to dispose of him.

He had read somewhere that Stendhal, his one-time favourite writer, had collapsed in the street, been taken to a cousin's house, and had died. That was the way to go, the relative, whether liked or disliked, put in charge. And the point being, not that the relative was held in fond esteem, or otherwise, but that he lived two minutes away from the accident. Thus had chance favoured the great writer who had surely never seen himself as an invalid, had in fact survived the retreat from Moscow. It was therefore essential to possess not only a relative but a relative who would prove to be near at hand. Sturgis had a relative, a cousin by marriage, but she (not a capable he) lived in north London, whereas he was in South Kensington, as distant as it was possible to be. He had even considered moving, particularly on days when the smiles faded from faces after his all too valiant greeting. Surely north London would be more festive, under the Jewish influence? His relative had on several occasions impressed him with stories of how well she was regarded in the neighbourhood, how obliging her acquaintances were, how respected she seemed to be. These attentions had made her not grateful but, rather, imperious, as if the favour were hers. What confidence, he marvelled. He visited her for the entertainment value: his presence, on such occasions of display, seemed to be acceptable, although he suspected she disliked him, as being not quite a man, too given to flattery. His defence against this was his perception that she might be lonely, her local eminence a fiction behind which she took shelter, and himself a useful idiot whose job it was to subscribe to the myth. Exasperation was also present on these occasions, but he was careful to control this until he was safely on his way home. The indifferent faces of his fellow passengers on the bus consoled him, since these were in a way familiar. His lot was ineluctably cast among them, though he trembled at the prospect, for the habit of trust had been lost many years ago, and had in any case been fugitive.

Trust also meant faith, but this he had never possessed. Throughout the obedient years of childhood he had privately observed that God was unjust, or, even worse than that, He was indifferent. To the pronouncement, I am that I am, went the unspoken addendum, Deal with it. Boasting to Job of His omnipotence, His superiority to Job's peaceable sinless life, He offered no justification for any of this, merely issued a report. And Job had acceded, perhaps because it is preferable to be inside than outside, silently making his accommodation with the idea of injustice, of disproportion. And had been rewarded for his docility with the restoration of his fortune, as if he had agreed to let bygones be bygones. Perhaps he, Sturgis, might have been so tempted, had there been any sort of manifestation. That there never had been any such thing brought a certain comfort, but also an anxiety: was he not worthy? That was the feeling that had lasted, the true legacy of any attempt at a spiritual dimension to his existence. Thus he was truly bereft.

This Sunday, like all Sundays, was far too long. It was the prospect of the endless fading afternoon that had prompted the telephone call to Helena, his relative, the widow of the cousin with whom he had been on affectionate terms. He had felt sorry for her, knowing how difficult it is to live alone, thinking that women felt this more than men. He would have behaved towards her with all his customary, and customarily thwarted affection, had she not made it clear that his role was to be an inferior one, as a recipient rather than as an equal. So he usually resigned himself to a cool-headed appraisal of her folly (and of his), would listen to her accounts of her many

3

friends, among whom was one she referred to as 'my tame professor', and whose function in her life was unclear; there were also her partners at the bridge club – 'the girls' – and the neighbours who invited her to dinner ('They make such a fuss of me I don't like to let them down'). There was no need to reply to any of this, nor was there much possibility of doing so. He supposed that she received some reassurance from this recital. As for himself, it may have been something of a relief to spend time in her comfortable flat, to be served a cup of tea rather than to make one for himself, and even to note that this performance never varied. Yet he could see from her restless hands that she was as little at ease on these Sundays (and no doubt on other days) as he was, and that his visits served some sort of purpose. That, he supposed, was why they continued, were in fact seen as inevitable by both parties. They had respect for ancient contractual arrangements, if for nothing else.

And then he perceived the innocence behind such self-regard, the same innocence that fatally coloured his own character, his longing for reciprocity. He perceived it in Helena's boast of her own desirability, even more in her absolute refusal to give weight to his own life and habits. His presence in her flat was her only sight of him, her only knowledge of him: beyond these apparitions he was assumed to dematerialize. He knew that any attempt to discuss matters of general interest would be thwarted; even his health was a taboo subject, since her own would naturally take priority. He could see that behind her greeting, which was genuine, was the wish that he would not stay long. He also knew that when he was safely on the threshold, his scarf wound round his neck, she would bestow the same lavish smile, clasp his hand firmly, kiss his cheek, and urge him to let her have news of him. Yet when the door closed and he could hear keys being inserted into locks he sensed gratitude for his departure.

4

But each was the other's only relative, and somewhere in each consciousness was the memory of a family party or a celebration of some sort, now long gone. Tolerance was now the mode; there would be no sons or daughters round their deathbeds, a subject studiously avoided and valiantly concealed. Also they were the same age, give or take a few months, and in these latter days they would not altogether forgo one another, although they had become increasingly aware that love was lacking, or even friendship. This was an organic relationship, an attachment between survivors who happened to share one or two memories. In such situations feeling, or indeed sentiment of any sort, was secondary. Should either ever be so imprudent as to express sorrow or longing, an important breach in their civility would have taken place. So the polite pretence survived, more on his side than on hers, for he scarcely burdened her with a single thought of his own, knowing that her own preoccupations would occupy the time at their disposal, and each accounting the visit a success if nothing in the way of protest were evinced.

There was regret as well as relief in their leavetaking. They both knew that they might see no one until the following day, after a solitary night into which anguish had easy access. They made a mutual pact to behave well, though good behaviour was not now much appreciated. As soon as he left her dignified apartment building he imagined the smile fading from Helena's face, as it would now fade from his own. Out in the street he made a conscious effort, always, to straighten his back, so as to appear resolute and confident should anyone be watching. But he was in the darkness of a winter evening and there was no one about. He was frugal with money and rejected the idea of a taxi: he had never been an enthusiastic driver. Besides, the bus was more companionable, more democratic; he liked to share some experiences, though not others.

And urban landscapes had always thrilled him; he had spent all his holidays in cities, content with a glimpse of other people's domesticity. A child on a skateboard, an elderly couple arm in arm, a mother and daughter deep in conversation would furnish him with material for reflection, though this was sometimes unwelcome. Such sights were somehow more picturesque when noted in Italy or France, but even in England there were plenty of lighted windows into which he was careful not to peer, though he could not always prevent himself from stealing a brief glance. His habits were ineradicably solitary, a fact he could not hide either from himself or from others. Only Helena appeared not to find him out of the ordinary.

A car passing down the deserted street seemed to exhale a wistfulness which he was careful not to examine. This, he was aware, was not how a grown man, indeed an elderly man, should be feeling. Elderly men still had thoughts of love, even of passion, but he had loved too unwisely in his youth, and the experience had left him disheartened. As it was he no longer looked at women in the same way. His appraisal was offered not to those who were still attractive, but to those who were no longer beautiful and who had lost their assurance and their pride. His smile was invariably met with an air of scorn; he had learned that plain women are unwilling recipients of sympathy. At least with Helena there was no danger of mixed messages; they were resigned to each other, and although in many ways deploring their association managed a cordiality that might have deceived an outsider into thinking it heartfelt but which each knew privately to be short of the real thing. Indeed, waiting for his bus, as he always did on these Sunday evenings, he felt his good intentions fade, to be replaced by a sour resignation. But that he hastened to ascribe to this particular Sunday melancholy – the dark street, the unmoving lifeless trees, the unseasonable mildness – and invariably tried to look forward to the following day, when he would resume his activities, such as they were, with his smile once more in place.

What he admired about Helena, and would have liked to emulate, was her ringing endorsement of her own worth, or perhaps self-worth. His own reflections tended in the opposite direction. He was aware that despite the passage of time his failures were all intact, as if the primitive mind persisted throughout later events and came into its own in what must be the latter part of his life. 'We pass this way but once,' she would remark with a fine smile, while recounting a minor act of kindness – her own – to which he took care to respond with a smile of equal complicity. 'I keep open house,' she always said, when he complimented her on her hospitality. And 'I like to leave a good impression,' she said, when he told her she was looking well. Her appearance was on the whole good, if you ignored the thickening ankles, the thinning hair. In the course of the afternoon her left eyelid would begin to flicker, signifying weariness or fatigue, yet the hair was golden, the silk scarf arranged so carefully round her throat of fine quality. He also admired the unstinting formality that was his own preferred form of behaviour. Not only would there be tiny sandwiches, but also delicate linen napkins with which to dab the corners of the mouth, and, he guessed, an abundance of thick towels in the bathroom which he had never visited. And her tone gave such weight and substance to her often banal conversation that he was almost tempted to take her at her own valuation, halfway between pillar of the community and grande dame. This, no doubt, was how she impressed her neighbours.

Their regular meetings constituted a pretence, or rather a performance, but conducted without irony, and therefore honourable. Reality was very different, reality was solitude, a consciousness of being left out, of being uncared for. Reality for her was a matter of much vaunted popularity to which she chose to give credence, although he suspected that it was largely fictitious. Nevertheless she had stimulated her acquaintances into a guilty realization that she deserved attention of a sort, an invitation to dinner, an evening telephone call, at the very least an enquiry about her health. Reality for him was absence, colleagues with whom he had been on good terms throughout long unstinting years, friends who had moved away on their retirement and whom he no longer saw. Reality was above all his small flat which never managed to qualify as home. It had been perfectly adequate as a place to which to return after a day's work, but now that he occupied it all day it never failed to depress him. It was pleasantly situated, overlooked a wide palatial crescent of fine houses; the address was enviable, yet he had never managed to avoid a feeling of displacement from his original lacklustre home in Camberwell, though that had been far from happy, his parents tight-lipped with antagonism, and relief from their disharmony only to be sought in sleep, or in fantasies about the life he would lead when old enough to seek his freedom. Or indeed to leave home, though, strangely enough, home it had remained. Now those fantasies had been made good: he was on his own, in comfortable circumstances, yet intimately distressed by his inability to take these circumstances for granted, and uneasy, daily, until he could get out into the streets, in search of someone on whom to bestow his smile.

He had to admit that the flat had formed part of his early ambitions, his innocent snobbery. Crescent Mansions: the address had a noble ring to it, as if he were a character in Galsworthy or Conan Doyle. But, again, reality was different. Reality was above all his small silent back bedroom, which no woman had visited for longer than he cared to remember. This bedroom was the focal point of his disaffection, the room that disclosed his condition to him most readily. It had a quietness that any rational person would envy, but it made him feel helpless. If he cried out (but he would never do such a thing) no one would hear him. If he were taken ill there would be no one at hand, this despite the existence of neighbours with whom he was on nodding and of course smiling terms. But these neighbours were mostly young and went off to work every day; when they returned they had other activities, other friends to share their thoughts. Their sleep was no doubt untroubled, while his own hovered on the edge of nightmare.

And on Sundays the quiet was particularly oppressive. This Sunday was no different from all the others. A light rain had begun to fall, and for a while he stood at the window and looked out at the pavement. In due course he would scramble a couple of eggs. Then a blessed hour with a book – *The Great Gatsby*, which he was enjoying for the second or third time – and then bed. And somehow he would reassemble himself and gather his resources for the week ahead.

2

He supposed that there were others like himself who slipped uneventfully through their lives to an age at which nothing more was possible, that there were few choices to be made, and at which chastity was no longer a burden but remained a source of regret. 'You're too *nice!*' was the angry accusation hurled at him by the second of his two great loves, to whom his faithful attendance had proved stultifying. His bewilderment remained long after their affair had ended. He had thought his mild manners inoffensive, but it seemed that niceness was a shameful and unexciting condition, and that women were more likely to succumb to humiliating treatment, to brute attraction, or, at the very least, to some kind of provocation. But his goal had always been a domestic one, in spite of, or more likely because of, the lack of familial sweetness to which he had never become accustomed. Love and work: Freud's prescription for contentment was one he embraced whole-heartedly. He would have been a faithful husband as he had been a faithful employee. Even now the lure of other people's arrangements was hard to withstand; the lighted windows that tempted him seemed to invite not only speculation, though that was always present, but longing. His ever-present smile was an attempt to disguise his dismay at being denied so much. 'You're only so nice because you're repressing a great deal of anger,' this same woman had told him. He had said nothing, but for possibly the first time in his life had felt the anger of which he was accused. There was nothing he could do or say. Niceness was branded into him like a birthmark. And yet he had not sought it, and was somehow saddened by a condition which had earned him so few favours.

After that he had given up on the idea of marriage, the only state he was able to envisage, apparently disqualified by this disabling characteristic which was invisible to himself but glaringly obvious to others, to women in particular. He had filled his life with his work at the bank, where no one seemed to think him anomalous and where his undemanding steadiness was, if anything, an advantage. Colleagues, many of whom were congenial, had filled his days, making his return every evening to the flat less onerous than it was to become in the days of unwanted leisure. He did not even regret his early ambition to study art, although the Camberwell Art School was temptingly near at hand. His father had steered him away from its dangerous attractions and had put him in the local bank, which he saw as a prolongation of his undistinguished schooldays, not knowing that he had choices. In time he had graduated to a bigger branch in Victoria Street, where he spent the rest of his working life, subsiding into a sort of acquiescence which left his intimate dissatisfaction untouched. He had risen, modestly, to a position that ensured him a comfortable income, had invested wisely, and, long after the death of his parents, had bought his flat, and prepared to live what he thought of as a proper life. Occasionally, as he added cups and saucers, or a bedside table, or a comfortable armchair, he thought it odd that there was no one to share these activities, but looked forward to the day when he would no longer be alone. He had acquired girlfriends, for his hawkish looks promised a favourable outcome to each entanglement, and fell in love regularly, though never entirely wholeheartedly, longing for something more extreme, more transforming, than evenings at the theatre, dinners in restaurants, and visits to his flat which temporary company did little to enhance, until the day, or rather the night, when he was told of his failing, a character assassination that seemed to promise a lifetime of loneliness. The woman delivering the verdict had grown more and more angry, although he was the one who stood accused, and had eventually stormed out of the flat as if suffering from an insult. Slowly he had put the room to rights, and then, when there was nothing more to be done, had resigned himself to the following day. But he had changed his mind, had gone out into the deserted streets, and walked, glad of the darkness, feeling his bewilderment turn to shame, and grateful to have no witnesses.

After this spectacular and, it seemed, defining reproach he felt he had only two options. One was to cultivate the life of the mind. He had always been a great reader, and had found consolation in books. He joined the London Library, visited museums and art galleries, attended lectures at the Royal Geographical Society, where he met other regulars, at whom he smiled pleasantly, careful not to appear too eager to further their acquaintance. Even this activity was circumscribed. His fault, he had come to realize, was not only niceness but the wrong kind of desire: he brought with him an eagerness from which others shrank. Therefore he directed his attention towards such thoughts and appreciations which, though held in common, could be enjoyed in private. But this did not altogether satisfy him. Art, he felt, let him down. For great paintings he felt only respect. Museum spaces beckoned him in, even welcomed him, but then left him on his own. Religious subjects, in particular, left him desolate, while mythologies stirred him to dissatisfaction. Only in the shrewd eyes of a portrait did he find a certain resonance, and comfort only in the sight of fellow ruminants, immured in similar silence. A couple of tourists, planted in front of a picture and discussing it loudly and with animation, offended him, as if a vow of silence should be universally respected. Such visits took on the aspect of a duty, an obligation, although he was aware that a residue of acknowledgement, and of reference, was left. He persevered, and in time came to appreciate the exercise for its own sake. It did little to assuage his feeling of failure, maybe even exacerbated it. But, like fidelity, the habit became part of his nature, and he knew he would pursue it to the end.

He briefly considered the option of displacement, but finally dismissed it. Holidays were fine, but one had to return home, and he was not in a position to move abroad. His flat was unsatisfactory in many ways. The kitchen was too small, but he rarely cooked, preferring to pick up food from the Italian delicatessen near his office. There was that unhappy bedroom, once clamorous with denunciation, now lethally silent. But he knew that his dissatisfaction had less to do with the flat than with his own overwhelming need for sympathy, for consolation, which he carried over from his earliest memories of familial disharmony, from the lack of a warmth that was not physical, though that too had applied. And he had had his retirement to think of, when he would need landmarks in the long exile that would follow. In the event retirement was wished upon him earlier than anticipated. The arrival of a dynamic newcomer, some twenty years his junior, with ideas for new working practices, did much to discourage him from standing his ground. True to his nature he made a dignified departure, saving any rancour for his own private thoughts. He was, after all, well housed, well set up, and guiltily well off, though he was careful not to make this apparent. And he had his pride, which would not allow him to remonstrate. More than one of his colleagues regretted his departure: there had been a flurry of lunches, of meetings for drinks, until these had fallen off and finally all but ceased. He was careful not to ask how his successor was faring, and was, for this reason, thought to be happy with the situation. He found it easier, as time went on, to keep his own counsel, and in so doing earned a measure of self-respect. A slight edge crept into his judgements: he would indulge in exasperation, as others might confess to a mild addiction, and allow himself a more critical eye than he had formerly brought to bear on friends and acquaintances, sometimes taking an exquisite pleasure in perceiving flaws or inconsistencies that he had previously accepted without demur.

That left his final resource: contact with strangers, at which he was extremely proficient. These were the people to whom he was obliged to consign his fate; that was, in truth, the only option, the only one left to him. Fortunately there was no shortage of strangers; in fact everyone was a stranger. He gravitated towards the most humble of these: the cheerful Australian girl who cut his hair, the woman at the dry-cleaners who told him about her grandson, the Asian assistants at the supermarket. It did not surprise him that these were women, for women were the lost element in his life. Nor did it surprise him that he felt most comfortable with the fact that these were humble employees (though everyone seemed prosperous now). His own background was humble; his father had been a bank clerk, and had thus laid the foundations for his own more illustrious career. His mother had stayed discontentedly at home, in the gaunt house in Camberwell Grove, mourning the absence of her more successful relations, few of whom bothered to visit her.

Sometimes he was amused to realize how that dreary house figured so prominently in his own dreams and reflections. He could trace, without any effort, every cupboard, every door; his bed he remembered as the most welcoming he had ever slept in . . . In the same way he remembered friends whom he had otherwise forgotten, friends made in the unthinking days of childhood, and now completely untraceable. All that purposeful striving that had brought him to his present position he dismissed as irrelevant: he had followed an upward path and was left strangely tired by the ascent. Only his mother had seen that he might not be happy, but that was because she was not happy herself. She lacked company, notably the company of her own family, and a milieu which she saw as superior. Family gatherings were non-existent; only exceptional occasions, such as weddings, brought them together. And it was at such a wedding that he had met his cousin Roland's new wife, Helena, who was thus both a stranger and not a stranger. Like his mother he appreciated the occasion; more instinctive feelings hardly came into it. That was how the matter had stood for many years.

Socially unaware, as he had been then, he had been impressed by the waitresses speeding about the room in which the reception was held and had assumed that the bride was rich. In fact, as he was to come to learn, she was adept at acquiring help, and was to remain so. His cousin Roland seemed delighted with his choice, his bride slightly less so, as if merely acknowledging her due as a desirable woman. This characteristic had made his mother thoughtful, and the return to Camberwell Grove had been unusually silent. Never had their house appeared more joyless. 'You might write them a note, thanking them,' said his mother. His father merely scowled, feeling irked by the occasion, the parade of affluence. There had been little further contact, one or two invitations which his mother accepted eagerly, though it meant a journey across London and an uncomfortable evening of criticism from his father. Gradually the invitations ceased, and the next gathering was after Roland's funeral, which even his father attended. That was how the association had started, back in the days of what he thought of as real life, everything since appearing illusory. Again, feelings were neither here nor there. What was there, and indeed what was left, was a vague history, if only of years that had passed, and in which everything had a place, his house, his mother, himself.

3

Everything was cyclical. Reading this in Proust he had not quite believed it. Now he knew it to be true.

Every night now he put himself to sleep by mentally wandering through his old house, mounting the shadowy stairs to the even more shadowy bedrooms where a terrible silence seemed to reign, by day as well as by night. Sometimes there would come back to him a familiar detail, the creak of a wardrobe door, or the position of a water glass on his bedside table. Brought back to the reality of the present he would be momentarily surprised that he had ever disliked, even hated, that house, had longed to put it behind him, together with the melancholy that clung to its walls. He had thought it a fine thing, something of an achievement, to sell it and purchase this flat, as if to signal his emancipation from the past. Now he found that the past was not so easily dismissed, and almost welcomed its reappearance, seeing the present for the poor thing it had turned out to be.

For the present held its own dangers. Every time he listened to the news it was to learn of ever more disastrous mistakes. The other day, calling in at his bank with a query, he had run into an old colleague, with bad news of his own. Had he heard that Jenkins had suffered a stroke? And Babcock: Alzheimer's! Terrible! His wife was at her wits' end. He had sympathized, thinking uneasily of his own fluttering heart, his sudden onslaughts of fatigue, his occasional lapses of memory. He had sent his best wishes to whomever might remember him, and made as prompt an exit as decency allowed. The past then took on a welcome familiarity, something of his own, that could not be taken away from him until all the rest went. He searched his emotional landscape and discovered, much to his surprise, that all latter-day disappointments and humiliations paled into insignificance compared with that intimacy of association. Then it seemed to him a terrible thing to live without witnesses, as if he had failed to make good the inevitable deficiencies of both past and present, had never created a family of his own, so that he was haunted by a feeling of invisibility, as if he were a mere spectator of his own, his only life, with no one to identify him, let alone with him, in the barren circumstances of the here and now.

Was everyone of his age in the same quandary? He would have liked to discuss this with a sympathetic listener, someone with the same length of experience, the same references. An old schoolfriend would have been ideal, but in moving away he had lost touch. That was the worst of it: losing touch. And he had no brothers or sisters, no other relatives, which was an anomaly in itself. His only cousin, Roland, of whom he had been fond, had died young, leaving the widow with whom he kept scrupulously in touch. He made it his business to cultivate her, although she refused him access to her own life, and denied the reality of his own. It was the old dilemma: how was one to be known? He hoped in time to win her over, so that they might talk through such matters, such experiences. This, he was forced to recognize, was his need, not hers. She had created a web of familiars to people her apparent solitude. All he could do, in the face of her adamantine self-regard, was to lapse into amusement at such tactics. If she were determined to keep him at arms' length, he would bring into play his secret weapon, that edge of exasperation which had helped him, over the years, to criticize others almost as severely as he criticized himself.

And there was something ritualistic about that pilgrimage across London on silent Sunday afternoons that eased his permanent sense of obligation, though this was something he had fashioned for himself. It was a formality, and he was nothing if not formal. Also he was distressed by the obstinate lack of fondness between them: hers he could understand, while his own seemed graceless. Despite his assiduity they remained strangers to one another. She tolerated him, whereas he sought to please her. Without success. He thought she owed it to herself to discourage him, as she had no doubt discouraged men in the past. Perhaps his role was to remind her of her former self, although he had no knowledge of this. At Roland's funeral she had had a moment of weakness or faintness, and he had put out a hand to steady her. That had been their only physical contact. Nevertheless he continued to visit her every five or six weeks, though this was as much for his sake as for hers.

Less than her former life he was fascinated by the life she had made for herself as a widow. But he also took a stealthy pleasure in her domestic surroundings, her luxurious appointments. Her sizeable flat was filled with sizeable furniture; her kitchen, he knew, was almost big enough for a family. He particularly liked the small television on which she could watch the morning news while eating her breakfast at a proper table. Her bedroom, into which he had never penetrated, and never would, he imagined as a bower of self-indulgence, a tribute to her femininity, which seemed to flourish even without the presence of a man. Despite her age she seemed to behave like a thoroughly contemporary woman, regarding men as indispensable for providing certain advantages, and vengeful in her opinions if these were not forthcoming. He felt sorry for men in this unequal struggle. Women today, he thought, were as indignant as suffragettes, but their indignation had nothing to do with a desire for equality, rather the opposite. They wanted preferential treatment and were ungenerous if this was not forthcoming. They had acquired the upper hand and had learned how to play it.

Seated opposite each other on two massive sofas, the tea tray on a small table between them, they embarked on their ritual conversation.

'Well, Paul?'

'Well, Helena? How are you?'

She gave her usual deprecating smile. 'You know me – I never talk about myself.'

'Your friends? Your bridge club?'

'Well, that's rather fallen by the wayside, I'm afraid. I don't always get a lift, and I don't like being out on my own. I'm always looking over my shoulder. As you know, I'm a very vulnerable person.'

They both were, he reflected. At their age accidents could happen, were even likely. He studied her, saw that her usual immaculate appearance was a little altered, her lipstick a little crooked.

'But I've joined a book club!' she announced. 'A few neigh-bours – we go to each other's houses. And of course I get a lift there and back.'

'What a good idea. What are you reading?'

'One of Jane Austen's. *Emma*, I think. The book's over there. It's quite amusing. Do you get much time for reading? I sometimes wish I had more. But with my various activities . . .'

'Of course, you must be busy.'

'Oh, busy. Yes, I'm very busy.'

There was a slight pause. 'I've been thinking,' he said. 'I've been dreaming about our old house. You never came there, I think.'

'I can't remember. It was quite a journey, wasn't it? And

after Roland died I sold the car. He never liked me to drive myself. And before that, a long time ago, in fact, Daddy always saw to it that there was someone to drive me. As you know, before my marriage we lived abroad. The house in Spain, you know. That's where I took up bridge. Everybody played there. And then we travelled quite a bit. It was a good life.'

There was to be no answer to his questions. Some men, he thought, appreciated this sort of behaviour: his cousin had, obviously. It would offer no challenge to masculine pride, might even have flattered it. And there were the compensations: the high standard of care. Roland would have been soothed by the fine housekeeping, the attention paid to his comfort. He himself was almost persuaded that such a bargain, such an arrangement, could be justified. But it was light years away from the real thing. It was the sort of marriage that no romantic worth his salt could contemplate. There would be consolation in the prospect, but little sincerity. The absence, or loss, of sincerity might in the long run prove too high a price to pay.

Briefly he was reminded of his first time away from home, to escape the Blitz. He had been small, terrified, an unwilling guest in other people's houses. The image that remained with him was not of the discomfort, though that had been considerable, but of the impenetrable nature of the conversation. This was how it seemed to him now, as if he were constrained for all time to overhear a discourse in which he was to have no part.

'I'll make the tea,' she said. 'I'm sure you need it, after such a long trek.' She laughed merrily. But he noticed that she had some difficulty getting out of her chair, and revised her age upward, slightly. How old was she? Certainly a little older than he was, perhaps by a couple of years.

'Are you looking after your health?' he asked. 'We're told to take exercise. Walking is recommended . . .'

'I am rarely out on my own. As I say, friends drive me here and there.'

He gave up. 'I expect you'll want a quiet evening,' he said.

'Oh, one of the girls might look in. More tea? No? Don't let me keep you, if you have an engagement.' Another pause. 'How are you? You're looking well. You don't change, do you?'

It was significant, he thought, that she always asked him how he was at the end of the conversation rather than at the beginning. She was frightened, perhaps, that he might burden her with health problems that should – that must – be hidden from her. And from himself. Such confessions, such intimate alarms, for that was what they would be, must not be vouchsafed.

'I'm fine,' he said. 'Take care of yourself. I'll be in touch.'

'Thank you for the flowers. I'll look forward to hearing from you.'

She was relieved now that the visit was over, perhaps more so than usual. Once again he admitted defeat. The door closed behind him with an air of finality. Momentarily he feared for her, feared for them both. She, at least, would have company. He would be all too conscious of his small flat. He thought of himself as bounded in a nutshell, with the ever-present thought of bad dreams.

He bored her, that was obvious. But maybe she preferred the company of women. Women were supposed to be more merciful, or at least less critical, though he was far from convinced of this. And the girls, as she called them, might be loyal and ask after her admirer. 'Did your admirer come today, Helena? He's very faithful, isn't he?' And that would be the main advantage to be gained from the afternoon. Yet she was wary of him; they could both sense it. It was difficult to know how to justify his attendance in any other terms that she would understand. The sense of continuity, which he sought, between a populated past and a tiresome present, hardly constituted grounds for ardent communication.

Once the pains of love were relegated to the past the pains of living became more noticeable. He was aware of tiredness. And there was always a slight failure of nerve when the darkness settled in. Helena too must feel this. For all her self-regard, her unspoken demand for reassurance, she was old, and no doubt uneasy. These visits of his were of dubious value, apart from the status they conferred on her in the eyes of her friends, though he doubted that those friends would always be kind. He regretted, as he did so many times these days, the structure of the working day. Without that he was truly alone, a condition he would not allow to become pathetic, but a condition nonetheless which caused him much grief.

He would, he decided, space out these visits, confine them to a minimum. He would explain that he would be away for a while. In fact he would go away, away from the encroaching darkness that never seemed more palpable than when he was standing at a deserted bus stop on a Sunday evening in late November. He would sit out the Christmas hiatus in some southern resort. He would write to her when he got home. 'I forgot to mention,' he would say, and then consult his guidebooks. Christmas was no time to endure a make-believe family.

4

He decided on Venice, because it was not the obvious choice, and because he knew he would be comfortable at the Danieli. He justified himself, as he always did, to an audience of unseen critics. I spend virtually nothing, he told these people. And anyway I've no one to leave it to. As always he passed the test he had set himself, but by the narrowest of margins.

On the plane he helped the passenger in the adjacent seat to stow her various packages into the overhead locker. She thanked him profusely. 'Christmas presents,' she explained. 'Such a bore. But it's worth it to get out of London.'

'A relief,' he agreed.

'On holiday?' she asked him.

'Just a break for a few days.'

'Like me. Christmas, I find, is always a problem.'

He agreed again.

'Why Venice?'

'Oh, I've always liked it.' And one can be alone there, he added silently. 'You're going to friends?' he enquired. 'The Christmas presents,' he explained.

'Yes, one or two people to see. I'm staying with an old chum near the Accademia. Though she won't be there the whole time. I'll be on my own for the last few days.' She laughed merrily. 'That seems to be my fate at the moment.'

He wondered at her unusual expansiveness. Or maybe it was customary; he could hardly tell. In the course of the flight she told him that she worked part-time for a charity, that she was recently divorced, and that after the holiday she would be house-sitting for friends in Onslow Gardens. He forbore to tell her that they would be virtual neighbours, but felt something like anticipation. Her manner was restless, possibly festive. In normal circumstances he would have avoided her.

'Victoria Gardner,' she offered. 'Though everyone calls me Vicky.'

'Paul Sturgis.'

'Are you staying with friends too?'

'No, I know no one in Venice.'

'Oh, that's so sad.'

'Not at all. I rather like being on my own. I'm retired . . .'

'Lucky you. I can't wait. But I feel I'm doing something useful, you know. And anyway I can't always rely on my friends.'

For accommodation, he suspected. Or at least for hospitality. He stole a sideways look at her. A pretty woman, he decided. In her late forties or early fifties, blonde, well groomed, her appearance only just disturbed by that air of restlessness, her fingers constantly touching her earrings or sweeping back her hair. She seemed anxious to talk, although he gave her few cues. She seemed not to need them, to be used to conversations with strangers. As the plane prepared to land he returned her packages and wished her a happy Christmas.

'Oh, don't,' she protested. 'Don't remind me. I dread it every year. So dark and gloomy. And so many memories, not all of them pleasant. Thank you so much. You've been very kind to put up with me. Now I'd better face up to it.'

He handed her his card.

'Maybe we'll run into each other,' she said. 'Venice is such a small place.'

He agreed. 'No doubt we shall.' It seemed a civilized thing to say.

'Where are you staying?'

'At the Danieli.'

'Oh, wonderful. Have a pleasant stay.'

They disappeared into different water taxis, for there were more travellers than he had anticipated. As he was jolted across the dark waters he dismissed her from his mind. Or rather relegated her to the category of strangers to which she truly belonged. He did not expect to see her again.

Venice enfolded him, as it had done on previous occasions. The weather was dusky long before evening, and he found it appropriate to his mood, which was gentle, ruminative, peaceful. He breakfasted early, and set out to wander to the small obscure *campi* familiar from other visits. He would drink a cup of coffee in an unfrequented café before making his way back to the Danieli to buy a newspaper, or several newspapers. He did not miss his books: his concentration was reserved for the beautiful silence of the streets, in which it was not possible to regret the absence of company. The chatter of the woman on the plane would not be welcome in this atmosphere of calm, almost of estrangement. Yet, as he made his way back to the hotel for lunch, his newspaper still under his arm, he sighed slightly at the prospect of the afternoon ahead. To sleep was out of the question: waking in a dark unfamiliar room was too alarming to be contemplated. He would go out again, and sit outside Florian's, linger over more coffee, and listen to the music. Then, at a suitable hour, he would return, take his bath, and go down to dinner. Waiters were kind to him, respecting his good manners, his discreet appearance. He would take his time over the meal, reflecting that he had not eaten so much in months. He might drink a nightcap in a friendly bar, even walk again. He would sink into his large bed with a sigh of relief. Yet he was not lonely, or not more than usual. He was almost surprised to find that this desperate journey was after all turning out to be something of a success.

Then, as usual, he would go to the Accademia, despite his growing indifference to art and beauty. He would look, dutifully, at Carpaccio, registering only his own resistance to that calm distant universe, those pieties, that absence of judgement. The galleries would be silent, dim, empty and – for he knew himself so well – he would relinquish the task he had set himself, seeing it as invalidated by that same sense of duty that had directed his steps a mere half hour ago. He would re-enter the outdoor silence, feeling it no more companionable but more realistic, ensuring he would be forever confined to his own company.

On his last morning he took his seat outside Florian's and surveyed Venice for one final time. He did not think that he would come back. But the thought of his return to his dark flat, to the empty days and the ritualistic excursions, oppressed him like a malediction. He would manage, he knew: he had a lifetime's experience of managing, but this in itself was something of a defeat. He drank his coffee and prepared to leave, although the prospect of a further walk was not attractive. When he saw the woman from the plane crossing the great square he stood up urgently and raised his hand. Her delighted smile transformed the day.

'Good morning,' he said. 'You survived it, then? Christmas?'

'Only just. Oh, coffee. Yes, thank you.'

Without her make-up, without her earrings, she looked older. Her city clothes had been exchanged for a black T-shirt, black trousers, and a leather jacket. He thought she must be about fifty-three or -four, still a good-looking woman, but slightly careworn. For a moment he knew the pleasure of companionship, even if his companion turned out to be tedious.

'How long are you staying?' he asked.

'Oh, until the end of the week. I've nothing urgent to go back to. And then I'm house-sitting for these friends. I think I mentioned that?'

'Yes. Onslow Gardens. You don't live in London?'

'I live in the country, in Sussex. Shoreham.'

'I know it,' he said. 'I used to walk that way on a Sunday, when I lived in south London. Pretty place.'

'It's awkward. I love the house but it belongs to my husband. My ex-husband, I should say. He lets me stay there when he's out of town, which is much of the time. It's practically a time-share – that's why I escape when I can. He's expected back soon, and then I think we'll have to come to a more formal arrangement. He's been quite generous, but I think he'll have to see me settled. Properly settled.'

She pushed back her hair, in the gesture he remembered.

'Maybe you'll get back together again. It's not good to be alone.'

'You're telling me. He found someone else, you see. Oh, I could get him back, but why should I?'

To defeat the fear of dying, he thought, and found to his horror that he had spoken out loud.

She looked at him in surprise. Suddenly they were strangers again.

'You're not ill, are you? You don't look it.'

'No, no, of course not. I was being silly. What do you plan to do today?'

'Nothing much.'

'Will you have lunch with me? I leave tomorrow.'

'That would be nice. I'm sorry to talk so much. And you're easy to talk to.'

So others had said in the past, while he had been virtually silent. He recognized the pattern, but did not resent it. In fact he was delighted at this turn of events, which would give his departure an almost ceremonious twist. And he decided that he liked her, that she was a perfectly nice woman. Her story was certainly unconventional but in these deregulated days most arrangements were unconventional. He thought the husband a fool, instantly making allowances for any irregularities on her part.

As they strolled out of the piazza he felt at last like an authentic traveller, a man ripe for chance encounters, a man not excluded from good fortune. London seemed far distant, some way into the future. Yet for all the splendour of his surroundings, for all the knowledge he possessed of famous painters and writers in this very city, it was, yet again, the humble domestic detail that delighted him: a small reluctant child wearing too many clothes being propelled forward by a grandmother, or indeed his companion's own fascinating circumstances which he promised himself to look into. And Shoreham, which he knew well, having, as he told her, walked there many times on silent Sundays . . . Those Sundays, indeed all Sundays, he now rejected with a shudder. They had been his fate for so long that he had accepted them as a way of life. Now, suddenly, this no longer seemed to be the case. Bells tolled, pigeons scattered. Gently he took her arm. 'Shall we eat fish?' he asked. 'I know a good restaurant quite near here.'

Waiters, with perfect Venetian manners, seemed to celebrate them as a couple. He warned himself not to drink too much; he was in danger of succumbing to a fantasy. She was at least – or at most – twenty years younger than himself and a woman of whom he knew nothing. He liked the way she responded to an invitation, with obvious pleasure; he liked her broad smile. When she asked him what work he was in he was overwhelmed. In his experience women were not interested in one's work. And anyway he no longer had any work to bore women with.

'I'm retired,' he said. 'And before that I worked in a bank, which probably sounds very dull. But in fact I liked it, or perhaps it suited me. I liked to see people turning out every morning with their briefcases and their newspapers. Or perhaps I simply liked workers, or the idea of workers.' A quick glance at her told him that he had lost her. 'Tell me about your work,' he said.

'I'm dull too. I work in an office with three other women, three days a week. For African children with Aids. Can you imagine?'

'It does sound a little extreme . . .'

'The worst of it is that money – enormous sums; you wouldn't imagine – doesn't seem to make any difference to the problem.'

'Yes, that must be very disheartening . . .'

'I loathe it. I loathe the other women. If anything could persuade me to go back to my husband it would be the prospect of doing this for much longer.'

'Is that a possibility?'

'Oh, we talk about it. There are faults on both sides . . . I divorced him when he told me about this other woman. I could have got round it, but I'm afraid I wasn't too polite. He's not forgiven me, that's the problem.'

'Do you still love him?'

She looked at him in surprise and some annoyance. He saw that he had lost her again.

'Do forgive me,' he said. 'I'm forgetting my manners. Would you like coffee?'

'Thank you. And yes, I probably do still love him.'

She slumped back in her chair, clearly unwilling to pursue this line of enquiry, but also tired of it, as if the question had been asked many times. Women, he knew, displayed sympathy in these circumstances whereas he was merely guilty of curiosity. He could not imagine anyone divorcing for such a minor offence, any more than he could imagine exchanging a marital home for a life of expedients. Even his parents, grim and unhappy as they were, had remained faithful to the married state. At the same time he reminded himself not to be too thoroughgoing in his enquiries. That was women's work. His work was to pay the bill, which was now being proffered.

'This has been delightful,' she said formally. 'I was not looking forward to today. Or tomorrow, for that matter.'

'You know we shall be near neighbours when you are in London. Perhaps we could do this again. Or rather, have dinner.'

It was his turn to sit back, suddenly exhausted. This was entirely out of character. And yet this was how men behaved. Or at least young men did. He felt foolish. Nevertheless he gave her the number of his mobile, and said he hoped to see her in London. After that admission he was in a hurry to get away.

He was aware of the damp cold as they left the restaurant. It was winter, he reminded himself. He was not a young man, and he might be making a fool of himself. The prospect of his flat loomed bleakly. But, 'I'd love that,' she said. 'I'll give you a call when I get back to London, shall I?'

They shook hands formally outside the restaurant.

'Feel free to get in touch,' he said, as if he were still a bank manager and she a client. Then he watched her retreating back until it was almost out of sight, and eventually turned away to prepare his own departure.

5

The weather in London was unseasonably mild, milder, it seemed, than it had been in Venice, and dark without the expanse of sky and water, and the water's reflections, that gave Venice its air of nobility. The city seemed emptied of its inhabitants. Even the few shops that were open revealed depleted shelves, as if those who remained were held in contempt. Apparently it was mandatory to go away in the interval between Christmas and the New Year, and he had to remind himself forcibly that he himself had been away, so completely had his journey failed in its purpose, which had been to instil a sense of change.

The atmosphere in the flat was faintly minatory, as if there had been some failure of vigilance on his part, and as if change might be indicated by something outside his own volition. His own mild journey was now seen for what it was, as something timorous and uncertain. The flat itself was, as ever, unsatisfactory, and for a moment or two he indulged his fantasy of an alternative, filled with agreeable contents and different arrangements: a breakfast room, a scullery with a back door leading to a garden, a proper hallway with a proper hallstand, fireplaces in all the rooms. This was in fact something like his old house, the one he had been so anxious to leave. His mother, he remembered, had sat at a proper dressing-table, with its full complement of silver-backed brushes. People, he knew, still lived in this manner, in properly designed suburban houses, but one would have had to be born into a house of these dimensions, for he had no means now of acquiring one, nor indeed a need for one. But he revisited that old house nightly, in the hour before sleep, found his way up the stairs, hand running along the banister, or sat eating bread and butter at a long-vanished kitchen table.

In that somnolescent visitation, half memory, half fantasy, he recovered something of his youth, and indeed saw himself as confident, unquestioning, possessing for a brief spell a present and a future. 'You're so well situated here,' people said of the flat, which had once represented what he thought of as an appropriate solution to the problem of where to be, how to be. When invited out to dinner he would surreptitiously assess the comforts of other people's appointments, would long to move a lamp a little closer to a certain chair, replace the blinds with curtains. Whereas his flat, with its minimal advantages, its undeniable convenience, always struck him as alien. There was, he thought, not for the first time, an excellent Freudian term for his flat: *unheimlich*. That described it utterly. Quite simply it was not home.

Now the known world was fragmented, and he was displaced to this neighbourhood of strangers. His dreams were not so much romantic as territorial, a retracing of old paths. The same went for friendships, which, like that old house, were faintly anachronistic, like those lost friends of his youth, amicable witnesses to each other's progress, knowing without judging, humble, artless, literally so for those tastes came later. In that company, in those surroundings, he had once felt entirely safe, so safe that he was able to indulge plans of escape, and in due course to act on them. And by a circuitous route, which some might call destiny, found himself in this small space, his suitcase at his feet, as if his journey had been no more physical than yet another dream, almost a metaphor.

A card, which he picked up from the doormat, invited him

to New Year drinks in the chairman's office at the bank as it had done ever since he had retired. He would accept, of course, and, as ever, leave before vague suggestions about dinner began to circulate. He would be home before the real celebrations started. He never regretted his early departure, which had come to be expected. It was assumed that he had other invitations, a matter he did nothing to clarify. On such occasions he was his own best and worst company.

He had the impression that something in the flat had been moved, and spent a fruitless half hour searching for what it might be, until he realized that it was his own recent displacement that had lent his arrangements this air of unfamiliarity. He heard his young neighbour, who was something in the City, come crashing down the stairs on his way to work. Work! That was what was missing. At the age of seventeen he had heard his father repeatedly impressing on him the importance of work and had resented it. It was not perhaps the most benevolent advice to give to a school leaver. Moreover, he knew it was inspired by his father's disappointment with his own life. Now he was aware that the advice had been sensible; work had saved him, although he had secretly hoped that something more interesting would give his life colour and meaning. Love, he thought, and still thought, would do it, but in this respect he had been no more successful than his father. Sturgis loved women wistfully, and would make no distinction between them: all held the promise of fulfilment, and if this had proved illusory he still appreciated their confident worldliness, their apparent expertise in the matter of day-to-day living. The women he had chosen, and who had, in one way or another, decided against him, had been more far-sighted than himself, and had discerned in his unremarkable courtship the prospect of a lifetime of boredom, though he had thought to provide them with everything that they desired. But they had desired an excitement which he could not provide. Now he recognized that they had been right to do so. He kept no mementoes of the two associations that had meant most to him, understood that his own emotional legacy had been inadequate for the knightly quest that he had somehow set himself. Yet he remained curious, fascinated almost, by the minds of women, which, he reminded himself, even Freud had failed to penetrate, their combination of frivolity and determination, their absolute otherness. It was a pity that he had known so few women. A sister might have explained these matters to him, but there had been no sister, and the women he had loved had declined to play a sisterly role. For this he blamed himself, although it had occurred to him more than once that other men might secretly feel the same.

He thought briefly of the woman on the plane and hoped that she would not get in touch. His final impression was one of irritation, his own, and no doubt hers as well. By the time they had finished lunch he had decided that she would not do. She had no doubt arrived at the same conclusion. How could she not? She was still quite young and he was old; he hoped that his fatigue had not been too apparent, though she herself had looked disheartened. He had felt pity, but also some impatience. Her story of divorce, of homelessness, had been unconvincing: rather than sorrow he had been aware of a desire for revenge. He suspected that she was rather more in the wrong than she allowed, but was determined to play for sympathy as the more winning card. She was clearly not the sort of woman to live modestly; she wanted more, much more than she was allowed. If they were to meet again she would doubtless divulge more information about herself and her current dilemma, which came across as dissatisfaction, certainly, but also boredom. He did not intend to be kind. Some sort of reluctant sympathy had been drawn out of him, but he recognized this for what it was, the residue of unused feelings from earlier times.

The other person from whom he hoped not to hear was Helena, the pseudo-relative whose company he sought not for his own sake but, as he imagined, for hers. It was his duty, as a family relic, to make sure that she was still alive, and to do so with a show of cordiality. He knew that there was no sentiment in this; unfortunately the habit had been established and was now difficult to break, the cheerfulness with which he managed to greet her on those mournful Sunday afternoons steadily dulled by her own indifference. His task was to enquire, also steadily, about her own activities. His own were ignored. And yet he served some sort of purpose, enabling her to parade her self-sufficiency, and even to reflect, to her own advantage, on his assiduity. He was expert at disguising his own indifference, perhaps more expert than she was, and all the friends referred to must have assured her of her own success. The most searching question she had ever asked him was, 'What do you do with yourself all day?' With the best will in the world he could not ignore the fact that this was mildly offensive. To avoid answering he had looked at his watch, had given a start of surprise, had apologized for the brevity of his visit, and left, giving his well-practised impression of having people to see, appointments to keep. It was this question, if he were honest, which had motivated his excursion to Venice. Whatever indignation he might have felt quickly transmuted into sadness for them both. When he telephoned to wish her a happy New Year, as he was bound to do, he hoped that the call would not be answered, so that he could leave a message of fulsome good wishes which involved no loss of face. This call could be composed some time into what he still thought of as the working week, and his own activities, such as they were, could be resumed.

He decided to eat out, to behave like a tourist, which he felt himself to be, rootless, obliged to endure temporary accommodation. In that way his return to the flat might appear less weighty. He wondered what it would be like to live in an hotel, an occasional fantasy entirely at odds with the onerous reality of homes past and present. There could be a lightness to life if one declined to take it seriously, and what could be less serious than handing in one's key every morning before leaving for the day? This fantasy, by dint of being familiar, became the private life he had been denied. The hotel would, of course, be somewhere abroad, Paris to start with, and then Rome or Naples, always in the south, himself young, filled with energy and desire, and free, with a future of achievement still before him. Although he had never had the courage to envisage this as a possibility, he knew that a modified version of this strategem was not entirely unrealistic. What had once been a romance – a younger version of himself, with choices still to be made – could be turned into some sort of practicality, but there would be fatal shortcomings: he was no longer the young eager figure whose tireless ardour would send him out into the fascinating city, whichever it happened to be, but old, cautious, with a lifetime's deliberation built into him, easily, too easily, tired, still formally dressed, and with the same formality informing his thinking. His outlook now was irreversibly that of an ageing man, weighed down with the responsibility of being a paid-up citizen, obliged to care for his health in the absence of those who might once have cared for it in his place. That fantasy self, the one who lived without constraints, had no place in his thinking, and yet he sometimes liked to think of himself as a young man living only in the present, in romantic surroundings, with his desire to guide him. He knew no young men apart from this upstairs neighbour, whose pin-striped seriousness was destroyed every morning by his tempestuous descent of the stairs and his banging of the street door behind him, certainly not an artist, as Sturgis had once wanted to be before serving his life sentence in the bank. And now it was all too late, and perhaps always had been. Nevertheless he decided to eat out, as if there were some vestige of that rootless young man, the one who had never been, still in command.

During the dark months of the year this fantasy, on which he was free to elaborate, investing it with details of his own choosing, took on an autonomy, as if it were a work of art. It became as familiar to him as that old house. The two were somehow connected. This puzzled him until he realized that the life he had lived in the house and the unlived life he had created were antithetical simply because the unlived version was so superior to the reality. Paris, he decided; it would have to be Paris. And he could almost experience that uplifting moment of walking out into the sunlit street, his key left behind at the desk. The beauty of the imagined moment moved him almost to tears, so much so that he could, quite objectively, decide to put it aside in favour (but it was hardly a favour) of the familiar peregrination of old rooms and staircases, and wary of imparting this ideal to others, though that was hardly likely. He kept it secret, and when others spoke of holidays he felt no envy, sensing that his youth had not been wasted, because, had he the courage, he would have gained an experience denied to those holidaymakers, an experience that would have enabled him to enact further fantasies and to regain everything that he had lost, through inertia, through disappointment, and through a sadness that had become the very climate of his life.

None of this was relevant to his immediate purpose, which was to sustain such life as he unalterably possessed. This would involve buying food and making his depleted surroundings more engaging. But he felt a distaste at the prospect of tempting his own appetite, and it was with relief that he left the building and breathed a lungful of damp air. He would walk to Victoria, buy his newspapers, and find a comfortable restaurant. He settled on the Goring Hotel, largely because it was an hotel, though nothing like the hotel of his imaginings. He took a seat resignedly, ordered food for which he had no desire, and as ever, set himself the task of observing his fellow diners. These did not look promising. Two youngish men at an adjacent table had a brusque dismissive air, even when talking to each other; colleagues, he decided, rather than friends. They ate severely, intent on the reason for their meeting, which was obviously a meeting rather than a social occasion.

'Seddon will have to go,' said the older of the two.

'On what grounds?'

'Incompetence.'

'You can't sack anyone for incompetence these days. They invoke their human rights.'

'I'm prepared for that.'

'He can drag it out, you know, noise it abroad, become a professional victim . . .'

Good luck to him, thought Sturgis. He felt for the absent Seddon who was being plotted against in this well-fed and self-satisfied manner. He asked for the bill, having no desire to hear more. Something like this might have been at work in his own case had he not made his graceful exit. Although far from incompetent, he had been steady, all too reliable, and therefore boring. Institutions got as bored as people, he thought, and nodded pleasantly to the waiter as he was thanked for his usual large tip. Maybe it was not such a bad thing to be retired, he mused. The afternoon had lightened and he decided to walk home. After all, he had nothing else to do.

There was a message on his answering machine.

'Hello. It's Vicky Gardner – we met in Venice. I'll be at this number for the next few days. It would be nice to hear from you. I enjoyed our chat.'

6

At first he was annoyed at the interruption. He had been immersed in a reverie which must have had its origins in that familiar dream which took him by surprise with the sharpness of its detail. He had been back in the old house, although this time the house had a wider context, was grounded in the neighbourhood of his childhood, that unpretentious middle-class suburb with its row of shops that he could see from his bedroom window. The shops too were modest: a green-grocer, a chemist, a hairdresser, a dairy – not a supermarket in sight: they had not yet made their mark. He particularly remembered the proprietor of the chemist's shop, a portly, dignified man in a white coat, who never failed to enquire after his mother's health, and who had eventually been suc-ceeded by his daughter. As a boy he had known this daughter. They had originally met on their way to school at an even younger age, and thereafter to different schools as they grew older. In time she herself had graduated into a white coat, and served her customers with something of the gravitas she had inherited from her father. They still used each other's Christian names – hers was Patricia – but the original intimacy had had to be abandoned, for they were by now working, and therefore counted as adults, deemed to have acquired an adult demean-our. But he was surprised to realize that he remembered her vividly, both in appearance and in character, and for a while was acutely sorry to have lost touch with such a natural companion.

The innocence of those days! One grew to resemble one's

parents, taking on the lineaments of their features, imitating their gestures. Now, when he looked in the bathroom mirror, he was startled to see his mother's face looking back at him. But now the face was old, careworn, stamped with disappointment. That disappointment had come upon his parents naturally, with time, as it had in his own case. The interval of true innocence was, he knew, that brief moment before the onset of disappointment, which in his parents' case was compounded by loneliness. Why were they so lonely? They had few friends, and his mother suffered by comparison with her more substantial relations, in particular her married cousins. There was no apparent justification for this but it became an established fact: she was the object of their pity, for they judged that she had made a poor marriage, and it became clear that she had at times thought this to be the case. But now Sturgis thought that they had been happy enough, until they realized that they were alone in the world, without sustaining company. This was now how he himself felt. That was why he was drawn back to that remote time when, for all its growing sadness, he had known his place, when he was still able to raise his hand to Patricia as he passed the shop on his way to work, when she raised her hand to him in response, so that he could take his place at the bus stop with a residual sense of sweetness that derived purely and simply from the fact that it had its origins in the past. But it was a past that was shared, and that alone made it precious.

They should have married, he now thought. It would have been a marriage undertaken in all innocence, the same innocence that pertained to those early customs and surroundings. But just as the idea had entered his mind she had announced her engagement to the local doctor's son. Her father was delighted, and indeed it made a kind of sense. As for himself, he had not been heartbroken. Even at that stage she had begun to acquire some of her father's corpulence, and looked older than her years. Older, indeed, than he felt, with so many possibilities on offer. And they had lost touch, had lost sight of each other, and would never meet again, never raise their hands in acknowledgement as they passed each other on the street. That was what growing up did to some friendships, and growing older failed to redeem them. But somehow the memory persisted, in the strangest of ways, and she would appear to him in dreams, unaltered, much as she had been when first encountered, on her way to school.

This particular reverie, and others like it, left in its wake a residue of sadness, and not just sadness but distaste for his present arrangements – the dark little flat with its unknown, and, more often than not, transient neighbours, the slight panic that greeted him on waking to face another day, a day of conscientious goodwill towards people whom he would never entirely know, and for whom he did not entirely care. He was free, with a freedom he did not value, free to take holidays, and on a more mundane level to go anywhere at will, to take his meals away from home, without any forethought. But these freedoms were unattractive, and, he found, involved intense effort, in comparison with which going to do a day's work was simplicity itself. He had never quite admitted to himself that he too was lonely – he left that complaint to the truly derelict – but he longed for conversation, for some sort of exchange, for the sort of questioning he was able to lavish on others, not out of need but out of sheer curiosity. His careful appearance, his good manners, he was puzzled to discover, somehow acted against him, as if he were suspected of an unattractive intrusiveness. In the end this reduced him to resignation, as if he could no longer expect any further human warmth other than the small amount he had received in his early life and with which he must now

43

make his peace, the peace that very occasionally descended on him in the night, when he was fortunate enough to entertain some sort of company, and that mostly from the past. When the phone rang he had difficulty reconnecting with the present.

'Hello? Are you there?'

'Oh, do forgive me. I was distracted. It's Mrs Gardner, isn't it? How nice to hear from you.' He could hear himself becoming fulsome, remembered the arm he had eagerly raised to greet her as she came towards him outside Florian's and which had obviously given her the wrong impression. 'How are you?' he repeated, a little more formally.

'Oh, I'm all right. I find these days after Christmas rather depressing, you know.'

'You're not back at work?'

'Oh, no, the office is closed until after the New Year, thank goodness, but it does leave one rather at a loose end, with everyone away . . .'

'Why don't you come round for a drink? This evening, for example. We could talk about Venice. I believe you stayed on for a few days . . .'

'I'd like that. I'm quite near you, you know, practically on the doorstep. If you're sure?'

'Oh, quite sure. Two hundred Crescent Mansions. Top floor.'

Somewhat agitated, he removed a newspaper from the arm of his chair, went into the kitchen and retrieved a bottle of wine and two glasses, momentarily regretting that he had no champagne, with which, he supposed, it would have been appropriate to drink a toast to the New Year. But that would have been presumptuous, he reckoned: she must have more interesting invitations. His doorbell rang before he could entertain further suppositions, or even decide whether or not he was pleased with the prospect of this visit. He had thought earlier that he would devote the evening to Henry James, one of the later novels, which would entail scrupulous attention, a plan appropriate to evenings in which there was no possibility of distraction. When he opened the door he was not entirely pleased that he had uttered his invitation.

But she was an attractive sight, well dressed, fully made up, with the inevitable earrings in place, surrounded by an aura of scent, the same scent he had once bought for the woman who had castigated him for being nice, and which had lingered on the air long after her departure.

'Come in,' he said. 'How nice to see you.'

He led her into his pristine sitting-room, noticing to his surprise that it suddenly seemed almost comfortable.

'What a nice flat,' she said. 'Have you lived here long?'

'Perhaps a little too long. Do sit down. A glass of wine?'

'Lovely.'

The wine, however, did little to break the ice. She seemed glum, and he was once more reduced to harmless assiduity.

'No work at the moment, I think you said.'

'I'm going to give in my notice.'

'Oh, I shouldn't do that. Certainly it sounded rather sad, but any sort of work is valuable, at least I found it so . . .'

'I didn't always do my present job, far from it. I was an events organizer.'

Events organizer. It was one of those modern occupations, he reflected, like project manager, or indeed consultant, far removed from what he considered to be proper work.

'What did that entail?'

'Well, you know, organizing events. Launches for record albums, and so on. Gallery openings sometimes. Meeting interesting people.'

'It sounds very glamorous.'

'Oh, it was. Hard work, of course.'

'Of course.'

'I'm thinking of trying to get back into it, although with my housing situation so undecided this might not be the right time.'

He tried to steer her away from this subject. He had, he was surprised to note, little interest in her emotional affairs, although he could see that she was preoccupied, somewhat depressed. Instead he poured them both another glass of wine. He knew, from past experience, that she had no interest in himself and thought back with some regret to his lost evening with Henry James. But she had made the effort, and there was that reminiscent scent, which, despite its connection with past disappointments, suited her moody demeanour very well. The wine had brought a flush to her cheeks and enhanced her appearance. Anyone might have called her a good-looking woman, with her fair skin and hair, and a slender body, or what he could see of it, encased in a black pullover and longish black skirt. He was obscurely pleased that she was not wearing trousers, pleased too that she was treating this impromptu meeting as a formal occasion.

Outside the dark window rain must be falling: he could hear cars sizzling on a wet surface. So there was little point in suggesting that they go out for a meal, which would have provided a convenient conclusion to the evening. Instead he said, 'You're settled here for the time being, then. Quite a pleasant part of town, I've always thought.'

'Well, for a few months, I suppose. My friend is in New York for six months, which is quite convenient. In six months' time I could be anywhere. Anyway, in six months' time my husband might have seen his way to buying me a flat. Or a house. I'd prefer a house.'

'Oh, so would I. A proper house.'

'Only at the moment I've just got my allowance. He's quite generous, really, but it's not the same.' She touched her earrings, as if the gesture reassured her. 'I'd better pick up some food, I suppose. I seem to remember a shop on the corner . . .'

'Why don't you leave your shopping until tomorrow? It seems quite wet out. I could make us both some scrambled eggs. Would that be enough?'

She brightened. 'Toast?' she said hopefully.

'Certainly. And fruit to follow.'

It was the right suggestion, enabling them both to fill their respective roles, his paternal, or rather avuncular, hers prettily independent, but with an edge of melancholy which he could not help finding attractive. As they ate their meal he felt emboldened to ask more questions, and learned, in return, that she was estranged from her parents, who lived in Norfolk, but that this was not a matter for regret on her part, nor even, she thought, on theirs. 'I couldn't wait to leave home,' she said. 'I wanted my freedom. As soon as I left school I started travelling. That's how I met my husband, though that was much later, of course.' She flicked back her hair. 'Do you mind if I smoke? I know it's forbidden . . .'

'Do. I always found it rounded off a meal. I can't think why I gave up. I think I'll join you.'

They were now perfectly at ease. They agreed that Venice had been something of a let-down, relegated it to the past. 'Coffee?' he enquired.

'Lovely. One more cigarette and then I must go.'

To his surprise he found that it was ten fifteen. 'I'll call a taxi.'

'Thank you for a lovely evening,' she said politely, now younger than her proper age, which was, he supposed, around fifty.

'Thank you for coming. I'm so glad you got in touch.' This time he meant it. 'Perhaps you'll get in touch again?'

'If you're sure?'

'Quite sure,' he said.

7

The second encounter took place in the street, on a cold misty morning that seemed to promise an indefinite prolongation of an unyielding winter. With something of the exaggerated relief he had expressed in Venice he raised his hand to her and was delighted when she did the same. This was gratifying, though he warned himself to be prudent with such gestures, knowing that they were likely to be misinterpreted.

'How nice to see you. And on such a miserable morning.'

This sounded wrong, although he did not quite see what else he could have said. Again she made a pleasant sight, her cheeks pink with the cold, a child's woollen hat pulled down almost to her eyebrows. She looked young, younger than she had in her formal clothes. 'Where are you off to?' he asked. This too seemed wrong, but apparently the only way to avoid social gaffes was to opt out of society altogether, and he was not quite ready to do that, although woefully out of practice.

'Just off to see a friend,' she said. 'For coffee. I enjoyed our scrambled eggs evening.'

'You must look in again when you're not busy.'

'I'd like that. Must go now. Nice to see you.'

After the remark about the scrambled eggs he resolved to stock up with something more substantial, in case she did in fact visit him again, and made his way to the Italian delicatessen, where he bought supplies that would undoubtedly be out of date when this mythical visit took place, if it ever did. Yet somehow he knew that she would get in touch, even though he might never know when. He felt a certain lack of anxiety, which surprised him, and he hoped that she might feel the same. Nevertheless he went home with two bags of food, feeling as virtuous as a regular householder.

This illusion soon faded, and once more he upbraided himself for the promptness of his assumptions. Puzzled, he sat down and contemplated this all too familiar sensation. It was not even that he found her attractive, although he could see that she would be appealing, in a rather obvious way, to many men. The fault lay not with her but with himself. The fact was that all feeling for women had left him. This, he knew, was a lamentable side-effect of growing older: one concentrated on oneself, alert to the warnings from the only body one would now know well. This was akin to the loss of hope, even of faith, not faith in the spiritual sense, but faith in one's own ability to continue. He had enjoyed her company that evening, although he had found himself wary of the intrusion: the thought of how to end the event without seeming impatient had been at the back of his mind. And yet he had longed for an acquaintance for some time. A friend was too much to hope for, but a familiar voice, a familiar face would answer as much of a need as he was now likely to feel. And his eagerness in Venice, that urgent hand raised in greeting, and his pleasure at her answering gesture, could not quite be forgotten. He shrugged. This was all useless. He might see her in the street, but there were no indications that she might call again. Why should she? She had friends, and would soon find an occupation. Besides, as Proust's Swann had so cruelly observed, she was not his type. Nevertheless he stowed the food he had bought in various cupboards and resolved to spend the day away from the flat, out of range of any putative telephone call.

He walked out and turned instinctively in the direction of town, though he had little to do there. A call at the bank to check his investments and then, he supposed, lunch some-where. The day had lightened but was still overcast: it would be dark in the evenings for another two months. He was depressed by the state of the weather, as all those who had little contact with nature (now known as the environment, he reminded himself) were bound to be. Once more the vista of a warm lighted house came to mind, but he felt he had exhausted this illusion, and did not particularly wish to revive it. The reality was so other that he could not summon his usual smile for those few shopkeepers who purported to recognize him, even to count him as a neighbour. His particu-lar downheartedness had, he knew, something to do with Mrs Gardner, or rather with his instinctive preparations for a further visit from her. In truth he had no expectations from her company, which he would not normally have chosen. But she raised the ghost of eager preparations undertaken in the past, for other women, and for one in particular, for whom there could be no successor. This too had followed a pattern. Women, after pursuit on his part, had found him disappointing in a way he had never fully understood. His appearance, he supposed, was misleading: he was tall, and to all intents and purposes agreeable to look at, but his longing – for home, for love, for consolation – let him down. This became apparent in the course of intimacy, for which he could only blame himself. As to the source of this longing, he was still far from clear: simply he concluded that something was missing in his temperament. He no longer thought in terms of entitlement but supposed that his lovers did so, automatically, instinctively, and had decided that their entitlements were superior to his. They had not made a gracious exit from his life after the long welcome he had so lovingly prepared for them. This he had almost understood – understood their annoyance, perhaps, certainly understood their discomfiture. Although that had hardly matched his own. He had come up against a specifically female resistance which he could not hope to understand. Thereafter the idea of seeking comfort from a woman had bred in him a resistance of his own, and that in time became the essence of his disappointment. No woman now could remedy this, although a child might have done so.

He sighed. This thinking was retrograde and quite purposeless. He wondered at the persistence of such dark memories and reckoned that they were what kept psychiatrists in business. He was aware that there were many agencies that claimed to be able to relieve one of the past. One had only to read the more populist newspapers to be made privy to the sufferings of others ('My drink and drugs hell'), but who could believe in a cure, a fresh start? He remembered asking directions of an elderly man once in Paris, to be met with the words, '*Monsieur, il ne faut pas partir d'ici.*' That was the nub of the matter, a false start, an unsatisfactory continuation. Yet without a past, he thought, the present remained undefined, one's expectations frozen for all time, and random, without direction. As ever he thought he might have done better, even prospered, in another era, or even another place, where the natives, the citizens, were more helpful, more curious, and indeed more candid. He longed to have lived in one of those confessional novels he had read as a young man – *The Sorrows of Young Werther, Adolphe* – in which whole lives were vouchsafed to the reader, with all their shame, yet as if there were no shame in the telling. Here, now, one was consciously checked by a sort of willed opacity, a social niceness that stalled one's attempts to make real contact. The answer might be to go in search of that other place, and eventually to find an easy republic of manners in which one could communicate and be understood. Even so he wondered if this were possible outside the confines of a novel. Such a stratagem had been envisaged more than once, when he had found himself, unprompted, gazing longingly out of a window. It seemed as though the resources he had always sought in others were no longer available, perhaps never had been, and all that was left to him was another kind of exploration.

He found that he had reached Marylebone Lane, without having been aware of the streets he had passed through, went into a café he remembered and ordered coffee and a sandwich. He had no desire to go home, and indeed the day was now not unpleasant, had resolved itself into mildness, with a hint of better light to come in the months ahead. A walk would tire him sufficiently to ensure a good night's sleep, or rest without further introspection. His memories were in any case outdated, and he had no desire to revive those random sensations of familiarity which were of no use to him now. He set out to walk back across the park, and indeed found a sort of energy in doing so. As he neared Old Brompton Road he was made abruptly aware of tiredness but stubbornly continued. At the sight of a bookshop he felt a desire to be in a closed space and went in, though he had little need for more books. The books he remembered had nothing to do with the life he now led, yet they promised so much in the way of revelation. This too was misleading: revelation only benefited the teller, rarely his audience. Yet such revelations that stayed with him remained his only touchstone of authenticity.

'Anything I can help you with?' enquired a young assistant.

'Travel,' he replied, and was directed to a corner.

Vienna, he thought. Prague. Naples. And of course Venice. But he knew these places, which were in any case too famous, too important. What he was after was something smaller, a landscape, his own, from which he could view a mystical sunset, and where he might capture that fabled *rayon vert*, that brief streak of light before the darkness closed in. This would be entirely self-justifying, without relation to the past or indeed to the present, if that present were to consist of dull streets and closed faces, the present in which he was obliged to live his life, a life comfortable enough but without the enlightenment he had always sought. Back in the flat he surrendered to his own fatigue and would have slept, maybe even did so for a few seconds before being roused by the phone.

'Hello,' said a voice he was beginning to recognize. 'It's Vicky Gardner. Sorry I couldn't stop this morning. I was off to see someone who might help me with some work. No luck, however.'

'I'm so sorry,' he said absently. He had forgotten all about her, so intense had been his introspection.

There was a pause. 'I was wondering if you were in now. I'd very much like your advice. I'm sure you'd be the person to ask. The thing is,' she went on, but he interrupted her.

'Why don't you come over?' he heard himself say. 'I'm more than happy to help if I can.'

He reckoned he had perhaps twenty minutes in which to rest his aching legs, but remembered with relief that he had bought all that food earlier in the day and that now would be a chance not to let it go to waste.

8

'The thing is,' she said, 'I need some financial advice. You were in finance, I think you said.'

'I worked in a bank, so in a manner of speaking . . .'

He was wondering at what point he should put the water on to boil for the pasta. The salami and olives seemed to have disappeared: inroads had been made into the ciabatta. Mentally he substituted grapes for the sliced oranges with cointreau he had planned. His attention was claimed in a quite other direction.

'It's the same old problem,' she said, appropriating another olive. 'Where to live. My friend rang last night to say she might be returning earlier. That means I'll have to find somewhere else.'

'Is that a problem?'

'Oh, no, not really. I've got friends all over the place. They're used to me turning up. But I need to get settled. I need a permanent address. Then I can seriously get a job. I mean a serious job. It's not as if I were not qualified. I feel I have quite a lot to offer, you know?'

'I'm sure you have,' he concurred. He decided to leave the matter of her qualifications until a little later. He could see that she might be useful in some capacity: she was friendly and direct and might be a considerable adjunct to a harassed managing director in some business or other. She would make excellent contacts, since she had so effortlessly engaged him in whatever enterprise he was now supposed to address. Besides, she was attractive, and clearly considered herself to be an asset to any man on whom she might bestow her favour. His role would be a minor one, he deduced. He decided that any involvement on his part would be limited. In any case he had nothing to offer her in the way of financial advice, knowing little of her circumstances, which appeared hazy. The travels, the apparent ease with which she moved house, the fact that she had, as she said, a lot to offer, all struck him as unusual. On the other hand he knew nothing of peripatetic lives, could not even imagine being without obstinate memories, longed even now for deeper roots, for a more settled home, as if a future bereft of these questionable attributes were unthinkable, although they pertained more to dream than to initiative. Looking at her now he felt no more drawn to her than he had done when they met on the plane. Why then, outside Florian's, had it seemed a matter of urgency to make contact?

'It's my husband who's the problem, you see. I'm perfectly willing to remain on good terms but I need some sort of settlement if I'm to find somewhere to live. I think I'm entitled to that, at the very least.'

This was obviously a sore point. He could sense anger mounting, see colour rising in her cheeks.

'Before we go into details I'll just see to our main course . . .'

'Oh, this is more than enough. Don't cook anything for me. I'm on a diet anyway.'

'Some fruit, perhaps?'

'Lovely. The thing is I may have to take him to court.'

'Oh, I shouldn't do that. A court case could cost you a lot of money.'

'Not if I win.'

'And if you lost?'

Her bravado was unshaken by this observation.

'I'm entitled to compensation,' she protested.

'You said you were divorced. By mutual consent, I think you said.'

'Well, yes, in a manner of speaking. We're both strong characters. That's how it goes, doesn't it? We didn't always see eye to eye.'

'But compensation . . .'

'He hurt my feelings,' she said primly. 'Women no longer have to put up with that. That's what I mean by compensation.'

'Would money really compensate you? I can see that the wounds are still quite raw . . .'

He had come up against entitlements once again, these apparently being the property of women alone, women exerting their right to life, liberty, and the pursuit of happiness. It was entirely possible that this was a moral problem for which there was no solution. He felt a return of his old sadness at the thought that connections could be sundered in this way. He liked to think of friendships continuing unaltered throughout life. His own parents, ill-matched and uncommunicative, had observed this kind of loyalty, their covert unhappiness breeding in him a fierce desire for something finer, greater, an improvement on their flawed example, a success to alleviate their failure, and this had been his desire in all his love affairs; he could not understand how others could fail to feel the same. That this was an ideal did not disconcert him, rather the opposite. That this way forward in love was something higher than was natural selection was a conviction that had never left him, even if it contravened other interests – those famous entitlements, of which he had heard so much – and had made him, as a lover, more courtly, more chivalrous than was necessary. He had been made to learn that sex, once satisfied, was of little consequence, almost of little relevance to one's true instincts, that not everyone took the long view.

This woman sitting opposite him now, in her smart black accoutrements, could refer easily to other involvements, as if the transaction were understood to be temporary, as if everyone knew this to be the case. He felt humbled by his lack of understanding of these truths. For they must be truths, since so many people lived by them. It was a Darwinian process, he decided: will, energy, desire were all part of the same system, to be ignored at one's peril. He saw now what a dull lover he must have been, and in doing so, identified a shame to which he had never put a name.

'I'll make some coffee,' he said. 'This needs further thought.' He left the room, then turned back and added, 'Do smoke if you want to; I'll just remove these plates.' He could hear the fussiness in his voice, and was anxious to spare them both the evidence of this. He took longer than was strictly necessary in the kitchen, feeling sorrow not only on his own account – that was habitual – but on hers as well.

It was a blessing that he did not find her attractive for more than a few minutes at a time: he would, he knew, tire quickly of her assurance, her randomness. She was intriguing only as human company, as a momentary survivor of that same Christmas malaise as himself. And yet they had come together in that same random fashion he was inclined to deplore, and their odd encounters had made Venice appear less spectral, less disconcerting than it might have done. Back in London some of that feeling was lost: London, his London, was a place of solid, even ancestral attachments, few of which existed in the present. For a fleeting moment he remembered Helena, and their unsought companionship on winter Sunday afternoons. He winced with contempt for these routines, which he had found himself unable to break. He had left a telephone message of good wishes for her, and told himself that there was no need to implement these in person. Better by far to learn new lessons from his odd visitor, who seemed disinclined to let their acquaintance lapse. This, of course, was flattering, not really within the repertoire of his arrangements. Although he had been found attractive enough by women, he knew he had little to offer beyond his own conformity. But this stranger, who had sought his advice, seemed to regard him as a normal human being. Granted, she had paid little attention to him, remained engrossed in her own drama. This was as it should be, he conceded: she had a risky edge to her which precluded much enquiry on his part, although he could see that she might entrust her problems into his keeping. Fortunately he was hardly in a position to help her. She seemed prosperous enough, her rootlessness habitual and no longer a disadvantage. He added some chocolate truffles to the coffee tray, carried it through, and was entirely rewarded by the abstracted gourmandise with which she ate one after the other. This was how women gave themselves away, he thought. Most played with the notion of self-indulgence, whereas she ruthlessly made no excuses.

'Now,' he said. 'How will you celebrate the New Year? I'm sure it calls for some sort of celebration, though I'm never sure . . .'

'I might go to New York,' she said. 'When my friend comes back. Exchange flats with her. Seems as good an idea as any.'

'And work?'

'Well, I've got things to settle before then. The money situation. I might take advice when I'm in New York. I know a couple of lawyers there. They're probably used to the situation.'

'Indeed.'

So she would be gone as quickly as that. He felt a little disappointed. It was probably for the best, he thought: she had sized him up and found him not to her way of thinking. It was merely their circumstances that had brought them together. Now their circumstances would detach them from one another. And yet the city outside his windows was still and damp, much as Venice had been. They might have felt more intimate had they found themselves out of doors, in the silent street. Suddenly he could no longer tolerate his warm flat, longed to be in an unfamiliar landscape, with only strangers for company – that old illusion.

'I dread Sundays,' he heard her say.

'I believe most people do. I don't like them myself. I usually try to get out a bit . . .'

She was not listening. 'What I'd like, you know, would be a proper walk. Round the park, along the river, something like that. But it's so boring on one's own. Especially when you're used to company.'

He regretted that his company was not the sort she was used to, but made a valiant decision.

'Why don't we take a walk together?' he said cheerfully. 'That would take care of Sunday afternoon. And we could find a decent hotel for tea.'

The words sounded absurd, ridiculous. But he was rewarded by the sudden brightening of her expression.

'I'd like that,' she said. 'Then we could have a really good talk. I'd be so grateful.'

She checked her earrings, smoothed back her hair, glanced at her watch. 'I'll check in on Sunday, shall I? No, don't get up. I know my way by now.'

9

The weather was disconcerting: still mild, but with a lurid sun sinking low in the sky. At four o'clock it would be dark. Left to himself he might have wandered down to the river, crossed the bridge to Battersea, contemplated all the closed windows, and cautiously taken the long way back. Or he might have simply stayed in and read the papers. Sooner or later a sense of discipline would have driven him out into the silent streets, but when he peered out they seemed, as ever on a Sunday, particularly unaccommodating. He felt little enthusiasm for this excursion, but drew some comfort from the thought that she might not turn up. It was, after all, a dark day, and most people would take the opportunity to rest, even to sleep. He imagined Mrs Gardner's sleep to be deep and untroubled, as befitted her robust constitution which could withstand disruption of all sorts, displacements, changes of direction, temporary derailments . . . Unlike his own which, after that ritual of reminiscence, was heavy, too heavy, so that when he woke it was with a feeling of alarm, that he had been absent too long, had missed a set of vital clues which might have guided his steps into the new day. No dreams: dreams were for the active, the creative. Hence his slight feeling of dread, every night, when he switched off his bedside lamp, only to be palliated by those memories of a time when he was equally at a loss, but not alone.

Mrs Gardner had almost entertained the same feeling of reluctance as his own, to judge from her rather set expression and her brief smile, which did little to convey acceptance.

'We don't have to go out,' he heard himself say. 'If you're tired,' he added.

'I'm not tired,' she said. 'What I want is air. I want a change of surroundings. I don't mind walking. I can walk for hours. It's just Sunday, you know? It always gets me down.'

'It might be different if one had some sort of faith. Any faith,' he said.

'Oh, I have faith. I have faith that someone is looking after me. That's why I never get fussed, you know? I feel that everything's going to turn out well, whatever I do.'

He did not have the heart to tell her that that sort of faith was entirely misplaced, that matters could change for the worse in a second. Only a few days previously, in the street, he had heard a woman murmur, 'I'm going to fall,' and she had in fact fallen, had lain prone, until concerned spectators had rescued her, until a waiter from a nearby café had brought a chair, into which she had settled with an air of bewilderment. He had continued on his way, but with a heavily beating heart, as if her fate were contagious.

'I hope you're right,' he said now. 'I envy you your confidence. Shall we set out?'

'If I could just leave this bag,' she said. 'It's much too warm out.'

'Yes, of course, leave it in the bedroom.' He wondered what was in the bag, but assumed that she was in the process of transporting her belongings from one temporary home to another. But it added to his feeling that she had not envisaged their walk as an end in itself, but had accepted the suggestion as a way of filling a dull afternoon. He wondered how enthusiastic her friends were to take care of her possessions, to give her house room when it was required, even to hear her story, not for the first time. He said nothing, anxious now to leave the flat, to have done with this encounter. His own discipline, he knew, was not a commodity that could be shared: he would have set out anyway, but her own tastes must be wildly different. Yet she tightened the belt of her raincoat with every appearance of alacrity, and flashed him a dazzling smile which held a hint of annoyance. This was so conclusive that he almost lost heart.

'Right,' he said. 'A decent walk, and then, I think, tea . . .'

'Where are we going?'

'I thought along the river, through the park, and then we could make our way into town, if that's all right with you. Just tell me if you get tired.'

'I'm never tired.' The reply, or rebuttal, was almost automatic. It formed part of her readiness, her disposability, her openness to another's plans. He admired her for that quality, so abysmally lacking in himself. It made him anxious to give her pleasure. The Ritz, he thought, or Brown's. She might like that.

They set out doggedly into the still silent streets, each regretting this exercise, which now appeared pointless. He would have preferred his own silence to the silence they seemed doomed to share. She too appeared recalcitrant, as if he were responsible for whatever disappointment she seemed to be experiencing. Instinctively he guided her in the direction of the river, dull and undisturbed in the afternoon light.

'Henry James lived there,' he said, indicating an anonymous red brick building.

She gave Henry James a passing glance, then relapsed into what he could only assume was a private conflict, one which excluded him and which he was in no way authorized to investigate.

'This must seem very boring to you, after your various travels,' he said. 'Where were you happiest?'

'South America,' was the unhesitating reply. 'I made my

way there as soon as I could. I stayed five years, or maybe six.'

'How did you live?'

'Oh, you can pick up jobs easily. And I made a lot of friends. That's never been a problem. I'm closer to my friends than I ever was to my family.'

'I've heard other people say the same thing. Maybe that's rather a fortunate state of affairs. Other people guide you through life in a way your parents might not have been able to.'

'And that's where I met my husband. In Buenos Aires. We travelled together for a bit. Then he went home and I carried on. I was quite happy. But after a bit I missed him. So I decided to follow him back to England – he'd given me his address – and eventually we met up again.'

'And married.'

'Well, yes, that was his idea. I thought we'd go back and carry on where we'd left off. But he turned out to be quite conventional. So I gave in.'

'And lived in Shoreham?'

She made a face. 'That was a mistake. I was out of my element, nothing to do all day. That's when I got in touch with my old contacts. Did odd jobs, much as I had over there. But it wasn't the same. Eventually I got into doing publicity for various outfits, spent more and more time in London, which didn't go down too well . . .'

'What did your husband do?'

'Worked in the family business. Property development. Well, there was nothing there for me . . .'

'I take it he was well off?'

'Oh, very. But I was bored. I was supposed to spend time with his family, his sisters mainly. But I've spent so little time with my own family that I wasn't going to take on somebody else's. As I say, he was very conventional. That's

64

when I knew I'd made a mistake. So I suppose I went my own way, got a bit careless. We more or less split up after a year. I went to New York for a bit, came back, went off again. In the meantime he got together with an old girlfriend. Who I *knew*. That did it. I wanted a divorce and I got one. Mutual consent.'

'Do you miss him?'

'I miss the house, oddly enough. And yes, I do miss him. He was my husband, after all, the man I know best. Maybe the only one I've ever known well.'

He suspected what she called 'carelessness', on her own part. She would not have taken this seriously. But he sensed a wistfulness, something of the wistfulness he often felt when he saw a man and a woman walking in front of him, heads together, deep in conversation. He believed her when he sensed that moment of longing, though it could be nothing as entrenched as his own. She was relatively young – but how young was she? – whereas his own solitude was lifelong.

They had walked along the river almost as far as the Tate, where he usually came to rest. Instinctively he raised his arm, summoned a passing taxi, and told the driver to go to Brown's Hotel. 'I've made you tired,' he apologized. 'But it was an interesting story. I hope I didn't ask too many questions. It's a fault of mine.'

She flashed him a brief smile. In the gloom of the taxi she suddenly appeared older. But he put this down to the bad light. He supposed she was an attractive woman, though not one whose looks he particularly appreciated. Not my type, he once again quoted to himself, and felt for her a certain pity.

The hotel, at least, was one of his better ideas. Soon they were seated comfortably in the warmth and the light, surrounded by the babble of voices, mostly American, and succumbing to the basic, almost infantile pleasure of eating food supplied by others. Once again he admired her unhesitating, almost abstract appropriation of sandwiches and cakes, noted enviously her unfaltering appetite. The sight of the food, and her almost disdainful pleasure, deprived him of any desire to eat much on his own account. Carefully he poured the tea. That, it seemed, was his role, just as it had been to listen to her narrative. Left to himself, he realized, he might have eaten more. He recognized the subsidiary nature of his own presence. Yet here was one of those strangers whose company he had tried to value: tried, but not quite succeeded in doing so. And she was pleasant, and interesting enough . . . As for him, this interlude was surely an improvement on time spent sitting in Helena's flat, asking the same sort of questions, or standing alone at the bus stop, hearing the echo of the door closing on him, the locks excluding him. Yet, for all that she had told him, he was as succinctly excluded from this woman's intimacy as he was from all the rest. He had supplied a moment of comfort, merely that. Yet he was pleased to see the colour returned to her face, a certain animation to her features, whereas before she had been shut off, almost mournful. He signalled for the bill. 'I'll take you home,' he said gently. He felt sorry for them both. They were glad to settle into the taxi.

'Where would you like him to drop you?'

'Oh, your place. I've left my bag there.'

'Of course.'

Suddenly he felt overwhelmingly tired. He wanted only to be at home, alone, surrounded by familiar associations. He wanted her, simply, to be gone. The corridor of his flat seemed longer than usual. He went ahead of her, switching on lights.

'You've got everything?' he asked. 'Your scarf?'

'Thank you for the tea,' she said. 'You must let me do the same some time. Or do you want to . . . ?' She indicated the bed. 'I could stay if you like.'

'My dear girl. Vicky. I am seventy-two, almost seventy-three. And you are what? Twenty years my junior. You deserve better, much better. But thank you for the compliment.'

At the time of saying this he felt little more than surprise. Gratification came later, when he was alone again. It meant little, he knew: this was current behaviour, at least he believed it was. He hoped he had not been ungracious. The truth was that such an offer precluded desire, at least for the moment. But, as he had found in the past, his refusal might lead to future antagonism. So easy an offer did not merit so principled a refusal. As the evening wore on, his feeling of gratification receded, giving way to familiar anxieties. How were they to meet again? Had he put them both at a disadvantage? Lying in bed, waiting for sleep, he wondered if she would now dismiss him from her thoughts, relegate him to the realm of insignificant encounters. He found himself uncomfortably aware that he might have offended her. He had, in the past, wanted to be kind, and, as ever, had supplied the wrong sort of kindness.

He had wanted to spare her the sight of an ageing body, foreseeing all too clearly the distaste that she would not quite be able to disguise. There was a great deal of discussion in the media on care of the elderly, but only the elderly could – but would not – reveal their own distress at what was happening to them. It was a matter of pride not to acknowledge the damage they were forced to undergo and to witness for themselves. He was briefly glad that he had no children whose lives might be overshadowed, even ruined, by attendance on him. Nor had he mistaken Mrs Gardner for some sort of daughter: she was too unlike him for that. She was, he had to admit, self-centred, incurious, whereas he sought information, some sort of connection, in every chance encounter. If the results of his approach had been disappointing he assumed that the approach was at fault, that he had been too effusive, had given offence in some way that he could not correct. But beyond this fault lay the greater fault of his decline, or what he supposed was his decline, his surrender of hope. Whereas she had probably thought of her offer as merely friendly, a way of thanking him for a well-meant if tedious afternoon, he knew, with the insight that age and experience had bestowed, that her true feeling would be one of pity, and that that pity would cancel her debt. So far he had been able to treat her as a simple acquaintance, met in odd circumstances far from home. It was true that she was showing signs of wanting from him something she no doubt wanted from everyone: help, the sort of help that does not content itself with advice. She wanted an audience, and he, as ever, had been willing to provide one. But he knew that his own need must be disguised, for to reveal it in all its sadness would be to lose any value he might still possess.

What he wanted from her was not so very different: not an audience – never that – but some sort of acknowledgement that he too had a life and a history, even if that was of no interest to her. He would have liked to be gently questioned, without in any way being judged. He would have liked to convey to her (or to anyone) the substance of those curious reminiscences that kept him company at night, while at the same time knowing that people of her age dealt in facts, not impressions, and tended to dismiss memories as undistin-guished as his own. To one who had travelled as widely and impulsively as she had, a life lived purely in the mind, as he seemed to have lived his own, would seem not only without interest but bizarre, unnatural. And it was not his place to tell her how this situation had come about. His mind would then appear as unattractive as his body. He supposed that he should credit her with some feeling for having made her suggestion, yet her gesture towards the bed had had a utilitarian element, like that of a waiter indicating a vacant table. He had been touched, but also displeased, as if this commerce had no place in his life, which was, he supposed, that of a disappointed romantic. Strange how a simple gesture could convey so many associations. That would have been one of the things he would have liked to discuss. But there was no hope of that now.

A short interval would be necessary before they could meet again without embarrassment. When some ten days had passed without a telephone call from her he assumed that she was angry, or, more likely, totally indifferent. He would have called her had he taken her number, or that of the absent friend, but this too he had failed to do. He supposed that he must now leave matters to chance, or to her own initiative, but found himself more than usually attentive to the surrounding streets, as if she might be seen at any moment. He remembered that at some point she had mentioned going to New York and consulting a lawyer friend there, and although he had dismissed this as idle talk he now began to wonder if she had taken off, as she seemed prone to do, without prior warning.

He could not help feeling that her absence, or at least her silence, was in some way attributable to himself, that he had failed to respond to what she had decided was an appropriate gesture. It had not occurred to her that his need was for company, or at the very least for conversation. He remembered with some amusement, and some affection, how she had consumed, with an abstract expression, so much of the food on offer, looking straight ahead, as if quite divorced from the process of digestion. And he was left with other questions, other unexplained characteristics: her indifference to her family, if it still existed. But did it still exist? This was one of the matters he would have liked to investigate. Only the knowledge that questions asked of strangers, as he had so many times sought and failed to do, were somehow out of bounds. This was not how matters were dealt with in fiction. There he had thrilled to the sort of full disclosure that the characters claimed as of right. Or perhaps the author did. But life, as he had discovered, was not like a novel. Or perhaps he had mistaken fiction for truth, or, more likely, mistaken truth for a more thrilling, more authentic form of fiction.

Never had the streets appeared duller, more uniform. There was a sheen of rain on the pavements, and in the damp air a promise of more rain to come. He wondered, not for the first time, how to use the day. He went through his usual procedure: the newsagent, the supermarket, the post office, all the while keeping a lookout for a familiar figure, with or without the bag of possessions that seemed to accompany her everywhere. When at last he thought he saw her he had immediately to correct his impression, for it was someone else, a much younger woman, seen only from the back. He wondered at this, blamed the bad light, yet even now was anxious to explore the nature of what he perceived as unfinished business. He had slept badly, but without those reminiscent explorations that usually preceded sleep, so that he was in some way doubly bereft of company. This was something of a relief, the one a consequence of the other, so that he was in some mysterious way indebted to her.

And yet he did not much like her. This was the bedrock of what he thought of as fascination, the fascination of a character encountered in a book. He regretted the questions he had not asked, but had respected her preoccupations as belonging to a quasi-fictional 'Vicky Gardner', who in the fullness of time would be explained to him. This, he was forced to conclude, was the extent of his attraction to her. Nothing could be less sensual, less sexual. He was interested only in the unfolding of the story, for he had no doubt that it was a story worth pursuing. That she would look askance at any such interest was clear to him. It was perhaps fortunate that he had remained so discreet.

When he did at last see her, quite by accident, it was across the street, near the tube station. She was not alone, was with a woman friend – at least he assumed she was with a friend for she was talking animatedly. He raised his arm, much as he had raised it that first time, outside Florian's, and after a moment, looking startled, she raised her own in return. He felt reprieved; now at last they might resume their acquaintance. He saw her return to her conversation with her friend, who seemed to be listening attentively, and stood for a moment looking at their retreating backs before going on his way, grateful that he had betrayed no undue attention. Just that raised arm, that gesture, so obstinately involuntary: the gesture that encapsulated their curious relationship, and which proved, and remained, symbolic.

The paucity of his contacts meant that information could come from no other source. But that in a way was satisfactory: the story must unfold naturally if they were to remain author and character. If he had any gift it was for private cerebration: why else did he strive to make sense of the persistence of totally unimportant memories? Because he had so few calls on his time or indeed his attention, he supposed. He was without illusions on this score, and the knowledge had in some way protected him against embarrassment, indiscretion. He was aware that he aroused little interest, and that when he asked relative strangers how they were, really wanting to know, their replies were tinged with forbearance, as if he were applying the wrong sort of code. At least he had not made that mistake, he reflected. She had been all too willing to tell him of her dilemma, so much so that he had little to do in order to elicit information. And he did appreciate the drama of her situation, albeit vaguely. It was what she was not disclosing that interested him more.

He was not entirely surprised when she telephoned that same evening, as if he had merely served to jog her memory.

'Hello, hello,' she said.

'How nice to hear from you. Would you like to come over for a drink?'

'No time. I just thought I'd let people know that I'm off to the States.'

'Oh, yes? For a visit?'

'I may stay longer. I've got friends there who can put me up.'

'I hope you'll look in before you go . . .'

'Well, I may have to. I'll be homeless as of next week. I wondered if I might ask a favour?'

'Of course.'

'Could I leave a couple of things at your place? I can't take it all with me: I'm travelling light. Nothing too bulky, just a small bag. Only the friend I was staying with is a bit of a control freak, and I don't want any hassle.'

'By all means.' This, it occurred to him, was the usual pattern of her arrangements. 'How do you want to . . . ?'

'I'll ring you some time before I leave. Then, perhaps, I could come over.'

'How long do you plan to be away?'

'No idea. It depends how things go.'

'You'll leave me an address, or at least a telephone number in case I need to get in touch with you? In case I go away.'

He had spoken on the spur of the moment. He had no idea why he had said what he had said. Yet the moment he had spoken a great longing opened up in him for space, away from this small hot flat, away from the tedium of his daily life. She had put the idea into his head, and he was grateful to her for having done so.

'Where will you be, then? Only if I need to get my things . . .'

'You'll be coming back? I will of course telephone you if you'll leave me a number.'

'Oh, don't bother. I'll ring you.'

'I hope you will. When do you want to leave your bag? I take it you mean the bag you had with you the other day?'

'Yes, as I say, nothing too bulky. I'll drop it in some time, probably at the weekend. I'll let you know. Must dash now: things to do, people to see, you know how it is.'

'Of course. I'll wait to hear from you.'

As he had done, he realized, for all the intervening days.

II

He was anxious now to be finished with this woman, who was, after all, a stranger, though not a stranger of the kind he envisaged – benign, efficient, professional – but someone whose presence was curiously unenlightening and in whom he was no longer inclined to take an interest. Indeed he remembered his passing inclination as misguided, rather more akin to hope than to love. And now he was forced to wait for her call (for she had still not left him her number) and to give house room to her effects, until such time as she chose to retrieve them. Her sojourn in New York would be open-ended, as all her arrangements appeared to be. Years at the bank had accustomed him to the precision of figures, had left him with a fondness for dates and times. His whole day was predicated on a kind of internalized timetable, devised by himself, unknown to all, but of singular importance in structuring the day. Without adherence to this structure he felt he might deteriorate into a more dangerous condition than his habitual melancholia, might realize that there was no need to go out, might even go back to bed and let the day take care of itself. That way, he knew, lay madness. Yet he had met people quite at ease with this regime, quite content to 'relax', to 'chill out', as they said: his cheerful hairdresser was one such. When he asked (for he always asked) how she planned to spend the weekend, he would elicit no more than a prospect of empty hours, which she seemed to view as the ultimate good. He supposed that she was able to contemplate this by virtue of a disposition which allowed neither doubt nor fear. Mrs Gardner too was of that number and therefore incompatible with one such as himself. This unwelcome assessment seemed to draw a line through his recent interest in her, which, though promising, had turned out to be misconceived. When she telephoned he would tell her that it would be inconvenient for him to house her belongings in his flat. He might be going away, he would repeat, and once again the prospect of escape presented itself as a real possibility. Yet he knew himself too well to set about making it real, looking, as always, for the sort of companion who would ignore his hesitations, and thus strengthen him for the foreseeable future. Until the end, he told himself, but dared not admit the thought to full consciousness.

He slept badly, was glad to bathe and dress, even to eat breakfast. When the telephone rang he answered resignedly but with a vestige of that hard-won resistance that had crept up on him, apparently when he was asleep, and to which he normally had little access.

'Mr Sturgis? Paul Sturgis?'

'Speaking.'

'We have your wife here. Mrs Helen Sturgis?'

'Helena. To whom am I speaking?'

'Oh, sorry. This is the Royal Free Hospital.' The voice seemed to come from a background of confusion, of female chatter. At one point it said, to someone else presumably, 'In a minute. I'm busy.' There was a muted protest. 'Well, hang on a bit longer. As I say, your wife was brought in a couple of days ago.'

'She is not my wife. A distant relative only.'

'She has you down as her next of kin.'

'What happened?'

'Apparently a heart attack. We're monitoring her closely.' The moaning started up again. 'When I'm not busy, I told you.'

'Who brought her in?'

'The caretaker. Apparently she was able to contact him. He called an ambulance.'

'How is she?'

'Well, rather poorly, I'm afraid.' The voice was raised. 'In a minute, I said.'

'I'll come as soon as I can.'

'Right.'

'Has she had any visitors?'

'No. So if you could come?'

'Thank you, Sister.'

'My name's Janet. We'll see you in a little while, then.' The voice was raised again. 'I said I was coming, didn't I?'

He put on his coat, picked up an umbrella, then put it down again. This was no time for encumbrances. In the street he was engulfed by an early morning crowd, which he never normally witnessed. Young people going to work, he supposed, all in competition for taxis. To his surprise he secured one, simply by stepping in front of a stocky young man with a briefcase who had already raised his hand. 'Do you mind?' he was asked angrily. He climbed inside and sat down. His mouth was dry. For possibly the first time in years he failed to register the weather, aware only that it was still dark.

The hospital struck him as disproportionately enormous, like the burial mound of an ancient civilization. Strip-lit corridors of immense length delivered him to a small ward in which he could not distinguish a familiar face. All seemed to him to be alike, wearing the same mask of bewilderment. Only one woman was sitting up, carefully brushing her hair. 'Nurse, nurse, can you help me?'

'In a minute. Hang in there.'

Still brushing her hair the woman addressed him. 'Can you help me? I need my clothes. I'm expected at home.'

'I'm sorry,' he said. 'I'll try to find someone to help you . . .'

'She's not going anywhere,' said a passing nurse. 'And you shouldn't be here. Can you wait outside?'

'Are you Janet? I was telephoned by someone called Janet. My name is Sturgis. Paul Sturgis.'

'Oh, yes. Over here.'

She led him to a bed occupied by a version of the woman he had once known, her immaculate hair flattened, her flickering eyelid still.

'Helen? You've got a visitor.'

'Her name is Helena. She won't answer to Helen.'

'There's no need to be aggressive, Paul.'

'How is she?'

'Well, as I said, we're keeping an eye on her. She was very agitated when she was brought in. She's calmed down a bit. If you could bring a couple of things for her? Washing things, you know. Perhaps a dressing-gown. Tissues.'

'Can she be moved to a private room?'

'I don't think so. We're looking after her. You'll find her keys in her bag. In her locker,' she prompted. He bent down and retrieved the bag, which he kept with him.

'You don't want to take that.'

'Yes, I do. I'll bring it back later, with the rest of her things.'

'You're not her husband, you say?'

'No, no. A cousin only.'

But he suddenly felt much closer. In this helpless gathering he almost felt himself included, waiting to be taken in. This was the reality against which he must exert his remaining strength. As he made his way out, aware of weaknesses not yet identified, a voice pursued him. 'Can you help me? I need my clothes. I'm expected at home.'

To be once again in the street felt like the order of release. Air! He wanted air! He felt surrounded by large implacable buildings, in comparison with which his own neighbourhood seemed situated on a gentle alluvial plain. This was nonsense, he knew, simply urban paranoia. But more than that: a curious homesickness, not only for familiar surroundings but for those very certainties on which his life was constructed, for the tedium on which he had come to rely. That tedium was now threatened. He was radically displaced, not only geographically but by what he had witnessed, by the image of that still stern face on the pillow, and by the echoing pleas of that other stranger in the opposite bed. As he had walked to the door he had noticed that she was still brushing her hair. He walked on, breathing steadily, as if his life depended on it, Helena's bag dangling from his left hand.

The flat was unchanged, with the same air of gloomy luxury that had half seduced, half repelled him the first time he had seen it. He opened the windows, looked round to see if anything were disturbed, but all seemed to be in order. The copy of *Emma* was where he had first seen it some two months ago. In the kitchen he washed up a cup and saucer, looked in cupboards, reminded himself to buy a loaf and some fruit, although there was little evidence that she would be capable of eating. The bedroom, which he had never entered, was as he had imagined it, exaggeratedly feminine, almost theatrically so. He took a light dressing-gown from the back of the door, gathered up a box of pink tissues, a toothbrush, a cake of soap, then, after a moment's hesitation, added a lipstick and a bottle of cologne. The bundle it made was small, but that would make it easier to unpack when she came home. If she came home, which seemed unlikely.

His task now was to find the caretaker who had been the agent of her removal to hospital. He made his way to the basement, knocked on a few doors, one of which was promptly opened, as if his arrival had been awaited. He began his introductions once again. 'My name is Sturgis. Paul Sturgis. Mrs Sturgis is my cousin. I believe you were kind enough to call an ambulance, Mr . . . ?'

'Crowther. Gave me a shock, I can tell you. I've got a bad heart myself. Doing all right, is she?'

'Difficult to say. I'm just going back there.'

'Only we've been a bit worried about her, living alone like that.'

'I believe she had good friends. She mentioned visitors. I suppose I was one myself.'

'I never saw any visitors. The wife looked in once or twice, took her a bottle of milk. Didn't like to question her. She was a proud woman, difficult to get to know.'

'Yes, that's true. But thank you. I dare say I shall be in and out, so don't worry if you hear noises.'

'Right. Give her our best wishes.' The door was promptly closed. This seemed to be a building in which the residents were armed against any intrusion by strangers. He had noticed the other doors, impassive, defying possible enquiries. He closed the windows once again, put the keys in his pocket, retrieved the handbag. Without the keys it weighed substantially less.

At the hospital he handed over his bundle to a nurse, younger than the one he had spoken to earlier.

'Is there any change?' he asked.

'Not really.'

'Is there anything I can do? I'll be back tomorrow, of course.'

'Can you come in the afternoon? Only the doctors do their rounds in the morning.'

'Of course.'

He lingered by the bed, arrested by a sudden access of feeling, or rather of curiosity. For this last relic of his family he was aware not of the conventional pieties he might have offered in the circumstances but of questions that needed to be answered. The drawn face, the unchanging stillness mocked the attention he was able to offer. What impressed him was a sense that her suffering would never end. *'Les morts, les pauvres morts, ont de grandes douleurs.'* When he had first read the line he had dismissed this as poetic licence. Now he was less sure. In comparison with what he saw in front of him, all artistic endeavour seemed futile, an attempt to engage with mortality and to win the contest. There was no choice in the matter: the contest was unequal. Even sorrow was an inadequate response. What he felt was awe, even dread. His poor life was still precious to him, inasmuch as he had arranged it for himself and in that sense had chosen it. He made no move towards the figure in the bed, too impressed to offer some sort of gesture, the touch of a hand. Even thought had to be postponed. He made his way out, raising his hand to a nurse, but she was busy, not too busy, however, to smile. That a young person could smile in the face of such dereliction struck him as miraculous. He gazed at her retreating back, thanking her silently for this evidence of a life still being lived.

12

Back in his flat he attempted to take stock. In the face of what
he had seen there was no place for Mrs Gardner, whose
situation now appeared both trivial and well rehearsed. The
question of her belongings was of no significance: contact
between them could be minimal and left in abeyance. She
would soon be gone, and he would, temporarily at least, be
spared her company. This was now seen for what it was, and
always had been: a diversion, an affair of chance, with the
initial charm of chance but with no deeper meaning. He
wished now that they had parted in Venice: he now had graver
matters to consider, and the effort of relating to those matters
was his, and his alone. The novelty of her company had
deceived him into thinking that it was merely company that
he wanted. Now he knew that this was an old longing that
could not easily be assuaged. They were, and would remain,
strangers. But it was the ideal stranger that he sought, and
would go on seeking, for close friendship still eluded him.

Present considerations were too serious. Helena, a woman
for whom he had little true feeling, as presumably she had for
him, had effected a radical change in his thinking. With her
demise he would be left without any vestige of family, however illusory that had proved to be. By virtue of bringing him
face to face with death she had somehow cancelled the past,
so that only the future remained. He would no more senti-
mentalize past attachments, no longer trace the memory of
the old house: a line had come to be drawn between past and
present, or rather between past and whatever time remained

to him. That that time would be grave he had no doubt: without attachments he would have to face it alone. Those strangers in whom he had put his trust might turn away, indifferent to his plight, and he would have only his own thoughts for company. And those thoughts, as he had intuited behind the mask of Helena's face, would be terrible.

According to the caretaker she had had few visitors. So that her accounts of her activities, her numerous and solicitous friends, may have been a fiction, as he had half suspected at the time. But the fiction may have served her well, allowing her a certain pride in her own resolute demeanour. In the need to keep up appearances they were as one, and yet at unguarded moments the truth would prevail. The locking of the door behind him had always sounded hasty, as if she could not wait to let down her guard. He was impressed and disturbed by this life lived according to stoic imperatives. Others, if there were others, would be equally impressed but for that very reason would not seek out her company. She had never worked, merely assisted her husband in some vague clerical capacity, and was thus deprived of colleagues, unlike himself. He had got on well with fellow members of the bank, had enjoyed lunches and invitations at Christmas, but these associates had moved on, had moved out, and gradually the invitations dwindled, and now he was not anxious to reactivate them. He had no children to boast of, and perhaps asked too many questions. Now he had lost contact, a state of affairs for which he blamed himself. But as to Helena, losing contact implied a deeper meaning.

On the following morning, after an uneasy night, he made his way back to the hospital. At the entrance to the ward he was met by yet another nurse, one whom he had not seen before, who said, 'I'm sorry. She passed away half an hour ago. We didn't have time to contact you.'

'I see.'

'It's no surprise, really. She was practically pulseless last night. Do you want to see her?'

The stark face on the pillow gave away no secrets, was in effect no different to the face he had observed on the previous day. He had witnessed other deaths – his father, his mother – but this one affected him differently. When his parents had died he had been a middle-aged man. Now he was old, and presumably the next death would be his own. He felt momentarily faint, and was aware of the nurse at his side.

'If you'd like to sit down for a few minutes?'

'No, no, thank you.'

'I take it you'll make the necessary arrangements?'

'Of course.'

Her address book must be in her bag, which was in his flat. That at least was his excuse for his precipitate departure. Only in the street could he recover himself. He managed to tell the nurse that he would be in touch and made his way out of the hospital, back into the blessed air, the sight of passers-by, of shops, buses, newspapers, and all the business of daily life. This was where he belonged, he told himself, and must resolutely belong. Even his own arrangements were now precious to him. There was a café nearby, and he went in and ordered coffee. But the business of eating and drinking did not proceed as normal: there was a persistent dryness in his mouth and throat which he could not ignore. After half an hour, his coffee untouched, he paid and left. He sensed a growing detachment from the everyday scene he had welcomed earlier. He must harden his heart, he told himself. That was the only way to survive.

For the rest of the morning he stood at the window of his flat watching two workmen unloading a van and moving several bulky objects into an empty house across the street.

83

He had imagined an alternative life going on in that house whose lights were on in the very early morning. Now there must be a new tenant whose belongings were being installed. What he watched was not the possible arrival of the new tenant but the workmen, whose unreflecting activity impressed him as a sign of real life, of a truthfulness that he was now, and only now, in a position to appreciate. Effortlessly they carried those boxes and indeterminate packages into the lighted entrance to the building, bending and straightening unthinkingly, unaware of the good fortune of a morning's dull work. He stood transfixed, following every movement, trying to appropriate something of their activity for himself. Never had he so longed to be humbly employed, to be told what to do. That was the essence of it: his own obedience being put to some good and painless use. The men, or what he could see of them, were not particularly young, were heavily built, but efficient. Soon the van was emptied, the street door to the building closed. The spectacle was over. With a sigh he moved away from the window and took up Helena's bag, his reluctant fingers searching for and finding her address book. He knew what he had to do, regretting, as always, that there was no one to tell him how to proceed. This was a useless regret which no longer surprised him, but was no less unwelcome, probably more so, for that very reason.

He searched the Yellow Pages, found an undertaker who would accept his instructions, stipulated that whatever ceremony they would arrange be the simplest possible. He confirmed that he preferred (the undertaker's word) cremation to burial. He then put a simple notice in *The Times*, and hoped that Helena's erstwhile friends, who had definitely existed, since their names were in her address book, might or might not see this, and that he was duty bound to inform at least one or two, who would could thus inform the others. When this was done he would consider his obligations discharged. The matter of attendance at the funeral could be settled, or rather expedited, as soon as the funeral directors got back to him. For the time being he did not want to talk to anyone. He moved back to the window, anxious for another glimpse – of something outside himself, but the street was empty. He realized with some disquiet that it was mid-afternoon, that he had not noticed the passage of time, that he had not eaten, and went into the kitchen to make a cup of tea.

When the doorbell rang he was startled, almost deciding not to answer it, but the habit of obedience was too strong. On the threshold stood Mrs Gardner, with a heavy coat over her arm and a bag at her feet. The bag, he saw, was much larger than the one she had originally carried.

'It's me again,' she said cheerfully. 'You very kindly agreed to give house room to one or two of my things.'

'You're off to New York?'

'Oh, tea! I'm dying for a cup of tea.'

'Do sit down. Though I must warn you I'm rather busy. I have to arrange a funeral.'

'Poor you. I hate that sort of thing.' She shuddered. For the first time he noticed a flicker of genuine fear in her eyes. 'Anyone close?'

'No. A distant relative.'

'Oh, well. These things happen. Still, I'm sorry. Shall I put these things in the bedroom?'

'Vicky, I have to know how long you'll be gone. I may be out, or away . . .'

'That's what I don't know at the moment. I'll keep in touch, of course.'

'When are you leaving?'

'Any minute now. I thought I'd better drop these things off before it gets too complicated.'

'Won't you want that coat? It will be cold in New York.'

'It's too heavy. And, as I say, I like to travel light.'

He sighed. 'Leave those things in the hall. I'll find a place for them later. The porter might have some room . . .'

'Oh, I'd rather you looked after them. There's quite a lot of good stuff in the bag.'

'Do you know where you'll be staying? If I need to get in touch. A telephone number would be useful.'

'Well, a friend will be putting me up. Don't worry. I'll keep you posted.'

'Your mobile?'

'Something wrong with it. I'll ring you when I get to New York.'

He sat back, defeated. 'What do you plan to do there?'

'Look up old contacts, for a start. See if there's a chance of working there.'

'So you plan quite a long stay?'

'It's all up in the air.' She scrutinized him. 'Is that a problem?'

'Well, I'd rather like to know . . .'

She smiled warmly. 'It's nice of you to be so concerned. But I'm used to looking after myself. Is there any more of that tea? Then I must rush.'

He had to admit that he was impressed. She was impregnable. How had she developed such self-sufficiency? Not once had she asked him the odd question. But that was her way, and he saw that it had protected her throughout a lifetime of ad hoc arrangements. After several meetings he still knew nothing about her. Her imperatives were quite alien to him: he did not understand her cast of characters, the mysterious husband, the nameless friends. Surely it was normal to divulge more information? In her position he would have been anxious to present some sort of guarantee of good behaviour. But that was not her way. He hoped she would be as good as her word and leave as soon as possible. When she showed no sign of this, he stood up. 'You must forgive me, Vicky. I have a lot to sort out, and it's going to take some time. I hope your trip is successful. I shall look forward to hearing about it. You'll be in touch?'

He hoped she would do no such thing. Again, this was unlikely. Once more he found her amusing, and by the same token disturbing. The contrast between her bright face and Helena's mask on the pillow was too striking. Of the two there was no contest. He would take pleasure – obviously – in the living over the dead. But as far as loyalty was concerned his duty lay in the opposite direction. He laid a hand on her arm, gently steering her to the door. 'Good luck,' he said. 'I hope it all goes well. But I'm sure it will.'

'Yes, I think so too. Thanks for the tea.'

When he shut the door behind her he shook his head in admiration. She had lightened the mood, for which he was grateful. He almost laughed when he stumbled over the bag, which she had left in the doorway to the bedroom. It was at least a sign that she would return, in her own time, obviously. And he would hear from her when she decided that that was in order, for she still had not left him a telephone number. He knew that his irritation would grow. He knew, decisively, that he did not like her. He knew that he could never love her. But she was an object lesson in how to proceed, and since that was his main uncertainty he thought her an acquaintance of rare value.

13

The formalities completed, he chose to consider the matter closed. A letter from Helena's solicitor informed him that she had left him her flat and the sum of ten thousand pounds. Other bequests had been to the caretaker, her cleaning lady, and to two people who he assumed to be her friends. Putting aside the matter of the flat for further consideration, he acknowledged that he was now more than comfortably off. He was touched and troubled by this bequest. He hoped that those Sunday afternoon visits had been of some comfort to her, but was not convinced of this. Apart from their tenuous connection they had nothing in common, were in fact two solitaries who saw themselves reflected in each other's eyes. 'Keep in touch,' they said to each other. This they had done, but without hope of intimacy.

One strange effect of these events was the cessation of his nightly reminiscences, his usual prelude to sleep. He realized that what he had so assiduously brought to mind – his hand on the banister, his seat at the kitchen table – was little more than a collection of sense impressions retained from childhood. These he now thankfully relinquished.

His growing irritation with his flat, now unavoidably complicated by Mrs Gardner's belongings, forced him to get up earlier and earlier. He tried to stuff her bulky coat into his small wardrobe without success. The bag remained unhoused. He was aware of its presence as soon as he woke, could not, even mentally, find a place for it. Bathed and dressed by an hour too early for any reasonable activity, he nevertheless went out, determined to remain out for as long as possible, to walk until the shops opened, by which time he hoped that his temper might have cooled. He set out in the direction of the park, which was desolate and unwelcoming, and sent him back to the streets, in which there was some evidence of life. The weather was still mild, but with a gusty wind and a hint of rain to come. His nerves were gradually calmed by the sight of young people going to work. That was his true climate, he decided: his former occupation, advising on investments, now bathed in a prelapsarian innocence, each day filled with mean-ingful activity, with acceptable company, and with a com-prehensible progression. At least it was all this in hindsight, but this version was preferable to the reality, which had contained its fair share of frustrations. He had never looked forward to the end of the day, had never anticipated the journey home, the moment of putting his key in the lock and settling down for the evening. This reluctance had been compounded by the idleness of retirement. He thought it must have been this factor that had let him indulge in the false nostalgia of memory. Whereas in fact, viewed without love or longing, as he was now able to do, he wondered if the past had been as protective as he imagined it to be, whether it might have been a false image of life as it might have been, had he had a more philosophical cast of mind. Now no rethinking was possible. He told himself that he still had his health, and in comparison with those elderly wrecks in the hospital this would have to do. In any event he was still active. To prove his point he would walk, eat out, not go home until he was too tired to walk any further. He would go to the London Library, seek consolation among the stacks, take out books that he had read before and would read again, find instruction and even corroboration in writers who, miracu-lously, seemed neither afraid nor ashamed to reveal their inadequacies, their disappointments, and whose very failures went some way to strengthen him in his long search for a fellow spirit, and, in the absence of such a spirit, for an understanding of his own life.

He walked to Piccadilly, which was properly awake, and went in search of coffee. He bought a newspaper, although he had one at home, and settled down in a small Italian café off Jermyn Street. He remembered buying scent for his mother's birthday at Floris, remembered too her reproaches that he had spent his money on such fripperies. He had not known how to coax a sign of pleasure from her, and had felt guilty for making her annoyed. He sighed, paid for his coffee, and left, finding some energy in his own annoyance at the recollection.

In Jermyn Street, on his way to the Library, he was calmed, as always, by the prospect of an hour spent in the proximity of books. What composure he was able to cultivate – and it occurred to him, ironically, that composure was the quality for which he was best known – had been the gift of all the books he had read, and, he supposed, would go on reading for as long as he was able.

He was pondering the merits of Henry James (too like himself in his hesitations and scruples) and Trollope (a diligent worker, also like himself) when he heard his name called.

'Paul? It is Paul, isn't it?'

'Sarah.' It was less a question than a statement.

'Do you remember me?'

'Of course I remember you.' I have never forgotten you, he added silently.

'How extraordinary to meet like this. But you haven't changed.'

'Neither have you,' he said politely. But she had, he saw, had grown older, and was marked by the process. 'Are you in a hurry? Have you got time for a cup of coffee?'

'Just shopping. And yes, I'd love some coffee.'

'Give me your umbrella. In here, I think.'

Seated, they gazed at each other like the friends they had once been, like the lovers they had also been.

'You're still beautiful,' he said eventually.

'And you're still nice.' *Too nice.* He heard the angry words again, the accusation that had remained with him since that time and had never lost its power.

'How long has it been?'

'Let's not think about that. At least we recognized each other.'

'You really haven't changed, you know. I have – oh, don't bother to protest. I've had a hard time, and it shows.'

He gazed into her face, with the privilege he had retained, and saw that it was true. She now wore rather a lot of make-up, whereas previously she had worn little. But the make-up failed to disguise a slackened jawline, an air of fatigue. He remembered her as a woman of decisive movements, staccato heels on the pavement, keys thrust carelessly into pockets. Now she was encumbered with an umbrella and a handbag draped cautiously over her shoulder and across her chest, which, he saw, was more voluminous than he remembered it. She must be in her late sixties, at an age that ushered in regret. And yet he would have known her anywhere. Age had altered them both, but their past intimacy reunited them, as if little time had passed since she had stormed out of his flat, infuriated by his forbearance. There was little sign of that now. She seemed genuinely glad to see him.

'Tell me about yourself,' he said. 'Tell me everything.'

She smiled. 'You always did want to know everything. Such searching questions! I felt quite intimidated at times. Well, there's too much to tell, really. And I hate the past, really hate it.'

'You said you'd had a hard time.'

'I've been very ill, Paul. After my husband died . . .'

'Whom did you marry?'

'There you go again. I married Richard. Do you remember Richard Crawford?'

'Vaguely.' He had a memory of a confident young man met at a party to which he had escorted her. Seamlessly she had transferred her attention, sensing someone more suited to her ambitions.

'Were you happy?'

'Yes, I think we were. We didn't know each other all that well to begin with – a whirlwind romance, really. But in time we settled down pretty well. And we had a good life. Richard was well off. There was no need for me to work.'

'Didn't you miss your work?'

'Not a bit. A woman never gets along too well in the business world.'

'That's hearsay, I suspect.'

'Yes, yes, I know all about that. But I liked having time to myself, planning holidays and so on. We had a little house in France, inherited from Richard's mother. Did you know he was half French?'

'I did, yes. I thought that gave him an unfair advantage.'

'It may have done. But I loved the house, almost as much as I loved him.'

These women and their houses, he thought. 'Have you kept it? The house, I mean.'

'Of course. And what about you? Still in that horrible little flat?'

He smiled at this return of her old asperity. 'Yes, still there. You said you'd been ill.'

'I still am. Or perhaps I've lost my nerve. That happened when Richard died. Ironic, really, since I was the one who was ill. And anyway we were no longer together. I was in hospital at the time.'

'Any children?'

'No. I had three miscarriages, and they left a certain amount of damage.'

'I'm so sorry. It's hard to have no children. I know about that. I always longed for them myself.'

'I remember that. I also remember thinking you were still something of a child yourself.'

'That may be true.'

'You never married?'

'I never married, no.' There was a brief silence which neither was able to break. 'How is your health now?' he asked.

'Poor. I have to rest a lot. I usually spend more time in France than in England, so it's the purest chance that we met like this.'

'I hope we can meet again. What do you like doing? Going to the theatre? The opera? I'd be more than happy to suggest . . .'

'I don't go out much,' she said. 'Not in London, anyway. Perhaps we can meet again like this. For coffee. I still want to know about you, you know.'

He saw that she was anxious to get away, her movements slightly agitated.

'Can I walk with you? Get you a taxi?'

'Yes, a taxi. I want to go home. Don't take it personally, though you probably will. It's just that I tire so suddenly I feel I might collapse.'

He glanced at her. She did indeed look tired. He stood while she retrieved her belongings. 'We'll find a taxi,' he said. 'Take my arm.'

They walked slowly, in the direction of Duke Street.

'Where do you live now?'

'Bedford Gardens.'

'And the house in France?'

'Near Nice. Saint-Paul-de-Vence.'

'I know it. A beautiful place.'

'Maybe you'll pay me a visit.' She was polite now, or maybe absent-minded, concentrating on her own condition.

'There's one. Do you want me to take you home?'

'No, no. I'm better on my own when I'm like this.'

He handed her his card. 'Please get in touch. If there's anything I can do . . .'

He watched the taxi disappear into a maelstrom of lunchtime traffic, regretting that he had not taken her telephone number. He doubted if she would contact him. He did not know if either of them truly desired a further meeting. And yet they had spoken without embarrassment, as if they were old friends. In truth, they were old friends, with more than a shared past behind them. If she did, by any remote chance, get in touch, he would be more than happy to see her again. They were both in need of company. He was surprised, heartened, by the absence of restraint between them. Of course that meant little in these days of easy exchanges. But perhaps it still meant something.

Love, at this age, was no longer possible. This he knew without a doubt. He had been made aware of the frailties of the body and had no desire to subject himself to further depredations. Nor, he suspected, had she. Neither would they want to engage with the urgent imperatives that had governed them in the past. Indeed, he viewed the idea with some distaste. The business of old age was wisdom and recollection. He hoped that she thought along the same lines.

In the flat, tired now himself, he stubbed his toe on Mrs Gardner's bag. He had the idea that he might simply transfer it to Helena's, now his, flat, and present her with a fait accompli. But that would be discourteous, against his nature.

He sat down, promising himself to review this as a possibility, but instead fell into a doze from which he woke with a start two hours later. He smiled. She had done him the service of giving meaning to a meaningless day, and for that, as much as for her company, he was grateful.

14

'I hate the past,' she had said. The remark had struck him as significant, and he was resolved, not without misgivings, to find out how much, or how little, that past related to himself.

This was their third meeting. They were in the same café, at the same hour, and both seemed acceptable. They were marked by the change in their circumstances, content to sit and gaze at people unlike themselves, in whose lives they had little interest beyond furnishing both a distraction and a welcome note of neutrality to their meetings. The weather was fine: commentators were reckoning that it was the mildest February on record. The passage of time before them seemed endless, the seasons unmarked. Sun penetrated the windows and reflected, or induced, a certain amiability. Patrons were few at this hour, most people being at work. Even the customary activity seemed to be in abeyance, as if it were already summer.

'Do you want to sit outside?' he asked.

'No, no. I feel the cold so much now. I never used to.'

'When do you go to France?'

'In a couple of months. It's quite an undertaking now that Richard is no longer there to look after things. I might even sell the house. I've had plenty of offers. And there are too many memories.'

'The past,' he prompted.

'The dreadful time I had with Richard's mother, who wanted everything kept as she had left it. I was relieved when she died. I never liked her.'

This was more like the Sarah he remembered, unabashed

at proclaiming her dislikes. That she had been able to do so freely in his presence had always struck him as evidence of a singular robustness, an ability to make unfettered choices. That had been part of her attraction: her fearlessness, although it had put an end to an association that had seemed to him to promise an inevitable conclusion. Although too sensible to envisage a happy ending, he had hoped that the signs were favourable. In truth he did not entirely believe that such an ending was possible; that he chose to put his faith in it was his misconception and his alone. And yet now that she was here, and that they were both able to reflect without acrimony, it seemed to him too good an opportunity to be wasted.

'I loved you, you know.'

'Oh, I know. It was not for want of hearing you tell me. I hated that.'

'Why? That was what I never understood.'

'You were a good man and you were wasting your time.' ('*Good*' seemed to be little more acceptable than '*nice*' in this context.)

'What did I do wrong?'

'You were entirely decent. Any other woman would have thought herself lucky, I suppose. I had other ideas. I was enjoying my freedom. I had a career, or thought I had. I had plenty of friends. I didn't like the idea of sole possession. It rather frightened me. As far as I was concerned you were just what I still thought of as a boyfriend.'

'I wanted more.'

'I wanted *less*. You were so courtly, so predictable. The dinners, the theatres: it was all so *stately*. Your idea of a good time was a long walk.'

'I must have bored you. I think I knew that at the time.'

'There was nothing I could put my finger on, just a growing feeling that we were incompatible.'

'You were right. I can hardly, at this distance, blame you.'

'There you go again. Why can't you call me names, lose your temper? I gave you enough reason to.'

'We wanted different things. I wanted stability. I wanted to come home to the same person every day. Every night.'

'You frightened me. I felt as if I were being taken over, made into something I was not cut out to be. That's why I was attracted to Richard. He never looked beneath the surface. That suited me perfectly. That was how we got along.'

'It sounds depthless.'

'It was. That was how I liked it. We had fun. We had the house, which we both loved. Although it was the house that became a problem in the end.'

'How so?'

'Richard's mother. A typical French matriarch. She insisted that everything remain the same, the way she had always done things. I couldn't even move the furniture. Richard thought the world of her. But we got across each other so much that I tended to raise objections to her. As she did to me. And Richard's death killed her, almost literally. In a way it was the only solution. And yet I don't feel the same about going back. Too many memories.'

'Your health?'

'My health is poor, Paul. I don't believe in morbid explanations for this. I was unlucky. Not that I was all that keen to have children – it was my mother-in-law who was keen. But I had a bad time and I'm still suffering for it.'

'You've changed in some ways, not in others.'

'Please don't tell me how. You would if you could, I know. But I've never shared your taste for analysis. And you must agree, most people get on well enough without it.'

'The unexamined life . . .'

'There you go again. I'm perfectly happy to meet like this.

98

In fact I think I like you better now than I did then, when I was merely in love with you.'

'Merely?'

'Oh, yes. Friendship, attraction, call it what you will, is easier to live with. And my state of health makes love seem so ridiculous.'

'Illness alters one's perception of other people.'

'It's not just that. I feel old. Well, I am old.'

'Younger than me.'

'Not much. I'm aware that I've made mistakes. I sometimes think of them.'

'I think of mine all the time.'

'Yet I still hate this sort of discussion we seem to be having. But I don't have too many friends these days, and you were always someone I could trust.'

'Are you lonely?'

She looked at him in surprise. 'What sort of a question is that?'

'The sort that wants an answer.'

'Well, you won't get one from me. I manage. That's all I'm going to say. Richard's friends have all been very supportive. They don't ask for explanations for everything. You always did. You still do. Are you lonely, indeed.'

'I sometimes wish that someone would ask me the same question. It would give me a chance to . . .'

'That's why they don't ask you. It would set you off for hours.'

'True. But I still think it's a question that should be asked.'

'Not by me.'

'I'm sorry if I've bored you.'

'You're not boring, exactly. Just something of a problem. But I do know that I can trust you. I always knew that. Now do you think you can find a taxi? That is what happens now. I suddenly run out of energy. Even talking wears me out.'

He saw that this was the case. Her whole appearance had changed, not solely because her colour had faded but because it was clear that her attention was focused on herself. He wondered if she were really ill, or, more likely, whether he had bored her, as he must have done in the past. And yet she leaned trustingly on his arm as he led her into the street, where she seemed to revive a little.

'Come,' he said. 'I'll take you home.'

For once he made no inspection of her surroundings, indifferent, perhaps for the first time, to houses and their contents. He settled her into a chair, went in search of a glass of water, which she drank gratefully.

'I've tired you,' he said. 'I'm sorry.'

'Everything tires me. Not just you, Paul. Don't stay. I'm sure you want to get on.'

'What will you do when I've gone?'

'Watch television, I suppose. Oh, don't look like that. I'll telephone you if I need anything.'

'And will I see you again next week?'

'Why not? And don't forget, if you feel like a break you can visit me in France.'

On his way home he decided that he was no more at fault than usual. He remembered that she was always adept at dismissing those whose company she no longer desired. He remembered her sudden changes of colour in the past and had thought them evidence of a powerful temperament. Now that she was no longer young she pleaded poor health, obtaining the same result.

'What do women want?' Freud had asked. And if Freud had no answer, what hope was there for the rest of them? He imagined legions of exasperated men asking themselves the same question and finding no answer. He felt a certain exasperation himself, and this was welcome. Surely women wanted to be loved – but why only women? Presumably Sarah had adapted to the needs of her own situation, had found the sort of man to whom she need not surrender her will. She and her husband had had a good time, as she said, without ever asking themselves if they wanted more. They had thus achieved a life which suited them, left them undisturbed, even undisclosed, and thus avoided the questions to which he was still trying to find answers. If there were any answers, which he now doubted. '*Monsieur, il ne faut pas partir d'ici,*' had said that man in Paris when he had asked directions. But to question his younger self seemed so retrograde as to appear absurd, distasteful. And for his present solitude he had only himself to blame. At least that was what his mother would have said. He had been impressed by Sarah's dismissal of her own mother-in-law, as if such attachments could be cancelled unilaterally. But she had always had the assurance, and presumably he had come into the same category as the tiresome mother-in-law, whose frustration with her son's wife had no doubt been as painful as rejection had been to him. It had made him excessively cautious, as if his own longing were at fault. Every woman he had met after that rejection had wondered why he had not lived up to his masculinity, his material situation, and had drawn her own conclusions, blaming them both, and for the wrong reasons. He had rejected the idea of marriage, let alone of a happy marriage, had realized that his basic desires would not be met, and had retreated into an amiable distance. This at least had had the effect of sparing him further accusations. In the face of such blandness no woman could feel justified in finding fault with him. He fulfilled certain requirements, and apparently required nothing for himself. The success with which he had effected this transformation made life easier, but did nothing to assuage his own solitude. To have no one to blame but himself, as his mother would have said, seemed to him a poor result for a life of unavailing effort.

Never had his flat appeared more inhospitable, as if it had received no visitors in decades. This was more or less the case. Only Mrs Gardner had found her way in, more or less welcome at the time but now appearing rather more of a nuisance than she had originally. He surveyed his sitting-room, which he had once furnished with a sense of entitlement, recalling the purchase of that chair, that table, as if he were at last his own man. The bedroom was and had remained disappointing, more so now that it was home to Mrs Gardner's bag. He had shared it intermittently with various partners, and notably, long ago, with Sarah. But those days were over; he was likely to remain undisturbed. That was the cruel fate of the elderly; he had seen it in Helena's pretence of social activity, which had revealed itself as nothing more than that. In truth the only person with whom he remained on equal terms was Sarah. With her he had a partner of sorts. They were still able to speak their minds to one another without causing offence. It was even slightly amusing to discover that they could recapture a certain familiarity. Without the burden of courtship he had felt a certain freedom in her company. Her invitation, careless though it had been, made a certain sense. Care would be taken not to annoy her further, just as she might in turn no longer wish to reproach him for the mistakes of the past, mistakes into which he had been led by the faults in his own nature. In the sun they might discover a friendship, or at least a friendliness that had been lacking. And if she were unwell he would minister to her – but not too much. It would be important to set limits to this. If he had to pay a price for his solitude he would see that in future it would take the character of independence. True solicitude, the kind he had made a point of showing to others, must now be redirected. This was a novel, even a revolutionary idea. He did not yet see how it could be implemented, but he would make it his business to find out.

15

He decided that he was not cut out to be a householder. Although he had always registered a strong desire for a space to call his own, the walls surrounding such a space were a matter of indifference to him, almost an irrelevance. Each arduous purchase had left him unsatisfied. Yet again, the idea of an hotel entered his mind. The ideal hotel, wherever it might be, should be in the centre of a great city. He must be able to step out into a radiant morning and return in the blue haze of early evening. After this vision the idyll faded somewhat, or perhaps imagination gave out. What business would he have in that city? How would the intervening hours be spent? Better, surely, to be safe at home, with no one to call him to account. Cocooned by an absence of witnesses, he was nevertheless in need of an audience, and of companions who knew him so intimately that he need never explain himself. Yet the image of anonymity, of which the hotel was the symbol, pursued him, much as his earlier memories of the old house had pursued him, until they died of their own accord.

The image came to him again, as did the conviction that he must change if he were to make his remaining time tolerable. How this was to be achieved was unclear. It came in the form of an energy which occasionally disturbed his habitual sense of loss. He had limited – very limited – choices. He could move house. He now had an additional property, and additional money. He could move into Helena's flat and discover a new neighbourhood. But he knew that he would soon become restless: the problem of the enclosing walls would soon return. He could marry one of the two women whom chance had put in his way. This had certain advantages, but equally certain disadvantages. If he married Sarah he would have to live with the verdict on his character which she had so unhesitatingly delivered. He would have to live with her poor health, whether real or imaginary, and thus condemn himself to a lifetime of care. This was well within his capabilities but no more attractive than his own condition, which, as time progressed, would claim all his attention. Or he could marry Mrs Gardner, with whom he was barely compatible. The advantage of this was nebulous but persuasive. Should any accident befall him – and this was increasingly likely, given his age – she would use her not inconsiderable initiative in contriving favourable circumstances, would commission doctors, specialists, private treatments, would appoint nurses, housekeepers, and thus to a certain extent care for him. His money would ensure her loyalty. This thought, grim but practical, seemed the more pragmatic choice, though he knew that both parties would enter into it with a reluctance that would soon become evident. He was surprised to discover that Mrs Gardner had the edge in these deliberations, though for the time being, since he was well enough to look after himself, there was no need to take this idea seriously. The novelty of her presence would soon translate into a subdued but persistent irritation. He had only to remember that he would never know precisely where she was to dismiss the matter out of hand. His memory was good, too good. The charm of their first real encounter, outside Florian's, had subsided quickly enough, and been replaced by various frustrations, the most tangible of which was the bag he had frequently to displace in his unavailing effort to disregard it.

This resolution was helped on its way by a telephone call

from Sarah, cancelling their next meeting. She was not well, she said. Obediently he made searching enquiries.

'Oh, don't fuss, Paul. I've been having bad nights. I don't sleep well.'

'Nights can be rather frightening. Do you take anything?'

'I have various pills, but they don't always work. They leave me rather disorientated.'

'I'm so sorry. Is there anything I can do? Anything you need?'

'No, no. I'll just have a quiet day.'

'Ring me if you need anything.'

'Yes, of course. I'll see you soon.'

'Well, you've got my number. I should go easy on the pills, if I were you.'

He replaced the receiver thoughtfully. The truth was that their idyll was over. Time had overtaken them both, and no pill could remedy this state of affairs. He remembered the vibrant woman she had been, impatient with his moderate manners, striding ahead when they were out together, and always sharp in her judgements. She had been striking, not quite beautiful, but beautiful to him, lithe, almost feral in her movements. She had seemed to him to be more in touch with nature than anyone he had ever known. Now nature had deserted her. Or maybe nature had taken over. Her nights, she said, were uneasy, she who had always slept like a cat. She had leaned on him, readily accepting his proffered arm. Her tongue was as sharp as ever; that at least had not changed. But the rest was subject to change, and its inroads were perceptible to both of them. They had passed the stage of knowing each other's bodies as intimately as they knew their own. Now they were victims of the secret disgraces of advancing age, and could no longer claim to know each other as they once had.

By contrast Mrs Gardner seemed almost unassailable, jetting across the Atlantic on a whim, living in other people's houses, and shored up by a sense of personal immunity which was an object of fascination. She would not suffer from night fears, and in her presence he would soon forget his own. She would dismiss his occasional weaknesses, look at him in surprise if he confessed to feeling tired, or perhaps not look at him at all, her attention permanently elsewhere. Her indifference would be therapeutic, a saving grace. He alone would know the truth of the matter, the calculations on both sides, and in due course these would cease to be relevant. And they had no memories in common, and thus no means of evaluating the past. There could be virtue in that alone.

A sign of his own advancing age was that he had begun to admire all the wrong qualities: vigour, triumphalism, egotism, and what was once condemned as brute force. These, however questionable, were unmistakably Darwinian, and more enjoyable than passive good behaviour. He now dismissed the injunction to turn the other cheek as mere foolishness. What purpose was served by selflessness, when, theoretically at least, it was possible to satisfy one's own interests? With the inevitable waning of physical strength came a corresponding desire to appreciate cruder qualities, particularly those he had never possessed, or perhaps had overlooked in his well-regulated progress through life. Sarah had been correct in condemning him as 'good'. Goodness was not an evolutionary goal. If he had succeeded in anything it was in fulfilling the requirements of others, as he had been instructed to do. Moral education was right to wage war on instinct, but instinct too had its rights. As it was, having resigned himself to behaving well, he was only able to appreciate evidence of more primal qualities in others. Sarah's undeniable willingness to condemn, Mrs Gardner's refusal to meet expectations he saw as safeguards. Both women exerted an attraction that was very nearly subversive. The spectacle alone deserved recognition.

Along with this discovery, or perhaps concomitant with it, went an aversion to anything which did not yield immediate results. The attraction, as opposed to the disincentive, of marriage, was that it could be done in record, or at least foreseeable time, so that the future would have a recognizable shape, would put an end to speculation and achieve a state of permanence. Not only that but a guarantee of safe-keeping. Along with this magical thinking came the conviction that his plan was entirely plausible. It was only when he examined more closely the characters of those involved that he knew that it was out of the question. But the realization did not bring closure. To be returned to himself seemed a condemnation of all his past. Yet this too was unavoidable. The shadow of a possible decision lingered in his mind, fantasmal though it now appeared.

Out in the blessedly normal street these considerations appeared ludicrous, as if prompted by an access of fever. He put them resolutely out of his mind, as if they had been suggested by someone else, some well-meaning but over-insistent friend. Neither of these women had shown any real feeling for him, and indeed he thought of them as strangers, as they now were. Fortunately they were both so absorbed in their own lives that they were likely to leave him alone. But alone he was all too free to contemplate an empty future, one in which he would probably need help of some kind, and in which, ideally, he could count on someone else to provide it. There was no solution to this problem. Even the prospect of returning to his old habits was now hedged with uncertainty. He could no longer tolerate his own company. Even the prospect of boring, and being bored by, somebody else, seemed preferable to the habitual sameness of his own thoughts. If only he could fall in love again! Only in that climate of urgency could he make decisions. But this was no longer possible. He was left with reason, which, at his stage of life, would propel him in directions which were uncertain, and which he would have to negotiate alone.

The weather was fine, his mood gradually adjusted itself to his circumstances, and he pursued his normal itinerary as unthinkingly as if he had been programmed to do so. He was free of obligations: that at least he acknowledged. He might ring Sarah, but decided not to. He was all too aware of her uncertain temper; with Sarah he still retained a vestige of pride which he was not inclined to forgo. They would no doubt resume their meetings in a week or two's time, resume too a certain sense of entitlement which they had always enjoyed with one another. There was too much in their past to be overlooked, but, he thought, a crowded past did little to relieve an empty present. That was his dilemma, as it was no doubt the dilemma of all those who reached his age, the age at which only one thing in the future was ascertainable. And that did not bear thinking about.

At home he settled down with a selection of books, not really inclined to read any of them. He was startled when the telephone rang, and more than resigned when he heard the familiar greeting.

'Hello, hello.'

'Vicky. You're back. That was a brief visit.'

'To tell you the truth it didn't work out as I had planned. I thought I might drop in on you if you're not too busy.'

'But of course. Come as soon as you like. I shall be in all afternoon.'

'I'm round the corner.'

'Then come straight away. I'll make some coffee.'

He had thought himself no more than resigned to her company, even amused by it, was almost grateful for the interruption. He was less grateful when he saw that she had brought with her a hold-all, slightly, but only slightly, smaller than the one encumbering his bedroom. He decided to make no reference to this: she might, after all, be en route to yet another friend, and he had no desire to put ideas into her head.

'So you cut your visit short?'

She pulled a face. 'People are so difficult, aren't they? So I'm homeless again.'

Yet she looked untroubled by this announcement. In fact she looked energized by it, on her mettle. She drank her coffee appreciatively, cleared the plate of biscuits, and lit a cigarette.

'So I got in touch with my ex. It's his fault, after all, that I'm in this fix.'

'Any luck?'

'No, not really. We'll meet for a drink some time. That was the best he could suggest. So I wondered . . .'

'I'm afraid not, Vicky. There's no room here, as you can see.'

She looked shocked. 'Good heavens, did you think I meant . . . No, it was just my things. I can't carry them around all day.'

'What did you plan to do?' His voice was gentler than he had intended it to be. She did indeed appear puzzled, as if not quite understanding his reluctance.

'Oh, I'm meeting up with someone I used to know. There might be a job in it. If not . . .' She made an expressive gesture with her hands. 'It's in the lap of the gods.'

'I've got a better idea,' he heard himself say. 'I know of a place where you can stay. Why don't I show it to you tomorrow? Then we can take your bags – both of them – with us. You're free tomorrow morning, I take it? Then I'll give you breakfast, and then we'll be on our way.'

16

'Where are we going?'

'West Hampstead.'

'Why?'

'You'll see,' he said, in the face of her obvious reluctance.
That she had not been in a good mood had been noticeable
since her arrival for breakfast. She had been late, which had
given him time to have the keys copied. Now, as he viewed
her set face, set in obstinate profile as they traversed London,
he acknowledged that the plan was his and his alone and might
not necessarily find favour.

'I own a flat there. You're very welcome to stay there as
long as necessary.'

'I don't know anyone round there. All my friends live in
central London. Chelsea. Or Belgravia.'

He had reason to doubt this, although her whereabouts
were usually a matter of speculation. However, she seemed
to turn up so regularly on his doorstep that he had to assume
that her headquarters, if she had any, were in the vicinity of
his flat. Somehow the subject was, or remained, out of bounds.
New York was the nearest she had ever come to a specific
location. Otherwise it had been a matter of staying with friends
who apparently had neither names nor telephone numbers.
Not that there was any reason why she should enlighten him,
determined as she was to retain her elusive status. He had to
admire her ingenuity. But this surely was an expedient that
was self-limiting: sooner or later she would be obliged to
reveal more about herself. Or would she? It was clear that she

was under no obligation to him, apart from voicing her needs from time to time and expecting an unfailingly sympathetic response. Initially he had found this entertaining. Now he was disappointed. He had contrived this situation as part of his desire to be more decisive, to be agent rather than recipient. He had even considered marrying her, although the idea now filled him with alarm. Yet he was hurt at this lack of reciprocity, of an acknowledgement, however insincere, of his good intentions.

'At least you will be able to get rid of your bags,' he now said. 'I'll sell the flat eventually. There's no rush, of course. But until I put it on the market you're welcome to stay.'

'I can usually find somewhere to stay. That's not a problem. And this is really not very convenient.'

'It's only a short journey into central London.' He found he was now pleading with her. 'Why don't you take a look round? The flat is quite comfortable. And you'll be free to come and go. Just let me know how long you'll want to stay. Ring me. Or I'll ring you.' It would be some sort of relief to be able to locate her. He handed over the keys. 'Let me show you round.' He paid the taxi driver, and, with a show of determination, removed her bags to the pavement. 'As I say, you'll be entirely free.'

The flat, which he had always considered well appointed, even luxurious, now appeared fussy, over-elaborate. The two sofas facing each other over a small table were designed for guests, for tête-à-têtes, but had probably received only himself and a very few others. The room now struck him as unbearably sad. Hastily he led the way into the bedroom, which was equally abandoned: no trace here of the normal life lived by an ordinary woman, no book on the bedside table, no radio, only the dressing-gown he had taken to the hospital and brought back again. Wordlessly he moved her into the kitchen:

here at least were some signs of domesticity. He felt diminishing enthusiasm for his plan, and from her silence he deduced that she felt none at all.

'Who lived here?' she asked.

'A distant relative. Now unfortunately . . .'

'You don't have to tell me. This place is like a morgue.'

'I'm sure you can make yourself comfortable.' Comfort was not in question: at least there was no argument about that. It was the general unsuitability that now struck him. This was no setting for a vagrant personality. It was even less appealing than his own flat, which at least had the virtue of economy. Here the air seemed to be eroded by over-large objects, by heavy fabrics. He saw it through her eyes and instinctively rejected it. Nevertheless he carried her bags through from the hall and placed them by the bed. 'I'll make some coffee,' he said. 'Then I'll leave you to get settled.'

'Can't we go out? This place is giving me the creeps.'

It was true that it seemed easier to breathe seated at a café table, in a mild sun, than in rooms which now struck him as dark, darker than they should have been at this time of year, winter beginning to yield to the distant but perceptible spring. The clocks would soon go forward, and then the impulse to move would return. Or rather to move on, as everyone seemed to say. Restlessness was not in his nature: perhaps he was becoming attuned to the restlessness in hers. He could see the attraction of being utterly feckless, free to change his mind, to become unreliable. But this too was a fantasy, and likely to remain so. It was entirely possible that the world had some vestigial need for boring characters like himself; in any event it was too late to change.

Silence fell between them. As she continued moodily to stare outwards at the traffic he realized that he had somehow offended her. That was the trouble with offering help: one came up against an opposing agenda to which one had no access. He noted that she had done little to enhance her appearance: her hair was listless, her face equally so. But her continued silence implied disapproval for his intrusion into her arrangements, though these remained nebulous. Apparently it was important to her to retain the right to being unknowable, untraceable. He sighed inwardly. He might venture some delicate probing, but then he would be back to his wearisome programme of boring interrogation, of engaging virtual strangers into exchanges about holidays, about their children – all the questions to which he usually reverted in his desire to initiate conversation, the illusion of familiarity.

'Tell me about yourself,' he now said. 'We know so little about each other. Or rather I know so little about you. I must seem like an open book: an elderly bachelor, living alone – not much to tell. Although everyone has some sort of story. Isn't that what they say about aspiring writers? Incidentally I doubt if it's true. Though some people seem more interesting than others. You, for instance.'

She turned to face him. 'There's nothing to tell. My marriage broke down. I'm looking for work. You know all that.'

'But before that? Your parents, your early life: that is so relevant. Do you have family? Forgive me. I've always been interested in people's early life. It shapes the adults they become. No one escapes their past.'

'Well, I hope I've escaped mine. I think I told you that my parents live in Norfolk.'

'But do you see them? I wondered why you didn't go home when you found yourself between jobs. Your parents must worry about you.'

'I ring them from time to time. We're not close.'

'Why is that?'

'Well, they always preferred my brother. He and I were

close. But he was ill, he'd had polio as a two-year-old, needed a lot of looking after. So I was more or less irrelevant. I took the hint, got out as soon as I could.'

'What happened to your brother?'

'He died.'

'I'm so sorry.'

She shrugged. 'It was a long time ago.'

'So, as you say, you got out.'

'As soon as I could. I got a job as an au pair in Paris. And after that there was no stopping me. After Paris there was no place for Norfolk in my life.'

'Yes, Paris does open one's eyes to the world. How long did you stay there?'

'Oh, about six months. I more or less had to leave; there was a certain amount of tension. So I teamed up with a girl I knew, in the same position as myself, and we moved south, worked in a café, that sort of thing. As soon as I had a bit of money I went off on my own.'

'That was quite brave.'

'She looked at him in surprise. 'Brave?'

'I shouldn't have had the courage. I always wanted to be in one place, and to fit in. And I had work. In the end work was what I came to rely on.'

'But you can always pick up some sort of work. At least I could. I was with a guy for some of the time – not the one I married. So I had someone to rely on. What I really wanted was freedom, the freedom to come and go when I felt the urge.'

'You mentioned South America.'

'Yes. I've always wanted to go back. As soon as my husband agrees to some sort of settlement I'll buy a house, rent it out, and go off again.'

'So any work now would be temporary?'

'Oh, yes. Work is only a means to an end, isn't it?'

'It depends on the sort of end you want. I valued my work, but perhaps it's different for a man.'

'I dare say.'

She had lost interest, although it seemed as though the glamorous past now had little currency except as anecdote. That having been offered, she apparently considered the matter of the past closed. At no point was there any sign that it had left an emotional trace. She had no inner life, it seemed. This to him was phenomenal, he to whom the inner life was all. Someone had warned him against such rumination, mocked him for his propensity to discuss it. Oh yes, Sarah. But he was on dangerous ground here and had no wish to incur the same sort of criticism.

'I take it that the flat is unsuitable? Or rather that you don't like the idea of staying there?'

'The flat?'

'The flat I've just shown you.'

She shuddered. 'It's hardly me, is it? All that furniture. All those *things*. And so quiet. Miles from anywhere. As I say, all my friends live more or less in town.'

'You could stay there until . . .'

'No. I don't think so. It was a kind thought. I might leave my things there for a day or two. Until I know where I'm going.'

He handed over the keys. 'I'll walk you back.'

'There's no need. If you're going home perhaps we could share a taxi.'

Alone he would have taken a bus, the same one he used to take after visiting Helena. He realized, with a grimace of irony, that he had been prepared to repeat the procedure on Sunday afternoons when silence became too much for him, or when dutiful cultural excursions lost their appeal. What else would transpire during those visits would be fairly predictable. And then he could go home to his own peace and quiet, and to his books. He gave a small choked laugh: magical thinking again.

'Are you all right? Look, there's one.' As ever, she did not wait for an answer to her question.

Obediently he raised his hand. 'Where shall I drop you?'

'Oh, drop me anywhere. I'll find my way.'

'Take care of the keys.'

'I'll let you have them back, don't worry.'

That meant another random visit, he understood. The matter was out of his hands. Just, he supposed, the way she wanted it.

17

He found somewhat to his dismay, but also to his considerable interest, that he had lost contact with his past. Only two memories remained, one of the old house, with its intimate geography, and one of his office at the bank, which had been his home for so many years. Both these places now appeared in a less friendly light. The climate of the first had been overshadowed by intimations of his parents' failure, of their disaffection. There had been no laughter in that house, few visitors to disrupt the mournful tenor of family life. All that remained was the decor of that life, one that he had been willing to abandon in favour of his first – and only – flat, which held no mystery and which now bored him.

As for the office, in which he had thought himself contented, this too was now overladen with all the evidence of missed opportunities, with what he now saw was his own cowardice. Those colleagues, with whom he had been on such cordial terms, did not, after all, have his wellbeing at heart. If he were to see them now he would be aware of their fundamental indifference, be aware too of their more richly furnished lives, their families, their children. He would not have sought their company, as he once had done, persuading himself that they were true friends. He saw now that they had indeed been friends, but of a careless unseeing type, friends who were unlikely to seek him out for the pleasure of his company. If he were to meet them now he would have had no difficulty in behaving with the same indifference, not wishing to go beyond the formalities that governed office life. There had been social encounters outside the office but these were purely functional: drinks parties, Christmas parties, frequent lunches, but with no intimacy involved. He had been in the background to their lives, and there was now no reason to look for more.

Of his schooldays he remembered virtually nothing. Holidays, undertaken eagerly as soon as he had achieved full employment, were a jumbled impression of museums, pine forests, and Baroque staircases. Only in later life was he able to discriminate, to linger, to observe. Even then he had seen himself in a romantic light, and although this was misleading the illusion had persisted. His love affairs were unsuitable, none more so than his love for Sarah, who came with a full complement of family and friends, lovers even, and whose careless assurance formed an indelible part of her attraction. Too often she had found him an irritant and had told him so. And had told him so quite recently, so that he knew that his memory was not at fault. Yet Sarah stood out from the past, was in fact part of the present. That he could not quite see her in the future he put down to his own propensity for introspection. At the prospect of redesigning his own nature he felt a familiar weariness, which he knew it would be his task to overcome.

He was not sorry to see his past for what it was but it had one morbid and disturbing effect: he no longer slept well. Without the comforting illusion of a context he could not ignore the fact that he was on his own and had always been so, and that sleep was no longer his refuge. He would wake suddenly, not knowing where he was, knowing only that he was adrift. In the hours of daylight he could dismiss his night fears, realizing that they were the baleful sign of old age, that they foreshadowed a death, which, though not imminent, was inevitable. For that reason he made strenuous efforts to live in the present, and sometimes almost succeeded. But the present was a poor thing without company, even poor company. Which brought him back to his resolution to make things new while he still had a chance to do so. And if that meant a change of direction which was not entirely to his taste that too must be envisaged.

He told himself that men throughout the ages had had such thoughts, had looked for some woman to take care of their needs, their comfort, even their safety. Quite simply he wished to put himself in someone else's hands. This was not entirely reprehensible: women too must think like this, particularly when they were no longer young. To abjure safety, to take risks was all very well when one was young, but that was no longer the case. What mattered now was to put an end to those night fears, to imagine comfort even in the teeth of the evidence. To become a conventional man now had its appeal. He would be able to look his former acquaintances in the face, be entitled to greet them heartily and without further desire to know them better. And if he had to say goodbye to certain cherished habits, to his solitude, his lack of responsibility, he thought that a price worth paying.

His desire to contact Mrs Gardner was destined to be thwarted. There was no answer when he tried to reach her in Helena's flat. This did not surprise him. He had nothing in particular to say, merely wanted to know if she had settled in, was comfortable. Her indifference, if anything, reassured him. She would not in any sense impinge on his consciousness, would remain a possibility, no more than that. She would, presumably, get in touch at some point. Or he would get in touch with her. They seemed to have established a connection which could be activated when one of them chose to do so, one based on his passivity and her needs. This was a novelty to him: he had never been so indifferent to a woman. The situation amused him. In fact Mrs Gardner amused him. It was only when he became aware of his detachment that he thought himself on unfamiliar ground. But this might have been a sign of emancipation from his former self. When he thought of his wistfulness in former love affairs he assured himself that this detachment was by far the better guarantee.

With a bit of luck this new decision – to change – could be postponed *sine die*, or at least until the summer. In the summer one was more optimistic, could plan journeys, feel one's muscles relax, banish thoughts of ill-health, keep mortality at bay. In the summer one let down one's defences, looked with pleasure at young faces, tried to emulate the unthinking confidence one saw in them. In the morose days that preceded this short annual apotheosis, there was little cause for joy. From his window he could see an orange plastic bag being blown by a considerable westerly wind: no temptation to go out. Yet he was restless, the consequence perhaps of his bad night. He contemplated making another effort to reach Mrs Gardner, but in fact telephoned Sarah instead.

'Sarah? How are you? It's Paul by the way.'

'Oh, I know it's Paul. How am I? Tired, very tired.'

'I'm afraid at our age this is pretty much par for the course.' Silence. 'Of course, you're much younger than I am.'

She gave a dry laugh. 'You haven't changed, have you?'

'I was wondering if I might take you out to lunch?'

'Any particular reason?'

'It's my birthday. I thought perhaps the Ivy . . .'

Another laugh. 'You'd never get a table at the Ivy.'

'Or the Caprice. The partners gave me dinner there when I retired. It was rather good.'

'I'm not sure . . .'

'Meet me there and I'll take you back. You won't have to do a thing.'

'Perhaps. I don't really like to commit myself these days.'

'One has to make an effort. Believe me, I know how you feel. But doctors say it's important not to lose contact. Sociability, they say . . .'

'I know what they say. I read the papers too.'

'It's important to keep one's old friends.'

'There aren't so many of them now.'

'So what do you say? . . .'

'I'm not sure. As I say, I've had a bad night . . .'

'Oh, come on, Sarah, you're not decrepit. All I'm suggesting is a couple of hours in the middle of the day. You're up to that, surely.'

'If it's your birthday . . .'

'It's actually my birthday today.' He had a desire to get this over.

'Happy birthday,' she said glumly. 'How many is that?'

'Too many. Let's not talk about age.'

'You brought it up.'

'Yes, well, I'm sorry about that.' He was, profoundly sorry. Having banished reflection he was not anxious to remember past birthdays, latterly spent alone, with nothing to mark the occasion. And he still, he found, wanted to see her. Perhaps he still loved her. In any event he was not inclined to let her go. That would be too easy. And even if he had no future to think of he was still determined to invest in the present. It seemed newly important to make changes to his life. And he knew that however unsatisfactory their meeting turned out to be she would still entrust herself instinctively to his care. Already he could feel her arm in his, her fingers in search of his own. 'Why not today? I'll book. I'll see you around midday.'

'All right.' She sounded surprised, not only at him but at herself. 'As I say, happy birthday.'

He was the first to put down the receiver, too exasperated

to do any more persuading. If it had come to this, he thought, there was little reason to carry on. But in the ensuing silence his annoyance subsided. It was simply evidence of their divergent responses to life. Their love affair had always been slightly combative, and that had been part of the attraction. It would be absurd to hope that nothing had changed. They had both changed, or rather been changed by the passage of time, a subject that could no longer be avoided, though avoid it they must, for the sake of their own endurance.

Perhaps they were not so very different, those two women. A certain obdurate waywardness seemed to be their prerogative. Despite their different backgrounds they seemed to come together in outlook and attitude. He was fully aware that in their eyes he lacked consequence. Not that they were entirely able to dismiss him; rather they were weary of his reticence, which might indicate a judgement they were not willing to undergo. Both had an insensitivity he could only admire.

On the previous night he had had a curious dream, from which he awoke bewildered. In the dream he was being shown over a flat by a friend who had heard that he needed more space. The flat was agreeable but in need of some repair. The rooms were larger than those he was used to. He had almost decided to take it when he noticed that the bedroom had no window. The implications of this, like the implications of age, were all too clear. If love were to die – and he thought of love in its widest, most comprehensive sense – then some part of him would not recover.

18

And yet this lunch was not going to be a success. He had known this as soon as he saw her, resignation written all over her features. To be sure she had made the effort she judged necessary: she was smartly dressed in a navy skirt and a striped jacket, and she had had her hair done, or he supposed she had, since it was drawn severely off her face and arranged on top of her head – no trace here of the careless looseness through which he had loved to run his fingers. Most alarming of all, she carried a stick on which she supported herself as she crossed the restaurant towards him. Rising from his seat he hoped that his face did not register the alarm, and, yes, the disappointment that he felt.

Surely this performance was out of place? She was not old, merely a once good-looking woman in her late sixties. He himself, he thought, was not much changed, grey-haired, certainly, but still upright. He rearranged his features into a smile of welcome, although he regretted this invitation, had in truth regretted it as soon as the suggestion had been made. He would have done better to have let the occasion pass unnoticed, have taken himself off somewhere on his own. Instead of which they were faced with a situation which neither of them desired, and he would be forced to see it through until he could deliver her back to whatever she would clearly have preferred to devise for herself.

'It's good of you to come,' he said, as menus were placed before them. 'I hope you're hungry.'

'Actually, I rarely eat lunch. But as it's your birthday . . .'

'I appreciate your making the effort.' For it clearly was an effort. 'Why the stick, Sarah?'

'It gives me confidence. I'm not really happy on my own in the traffic, crossing the road, and so on.'

'But my dear girl, you're not ill, are you?'

'I don't really know.'

'You've seen doctors?'

'Of course I have. They put it all down to the miscarriages, especially the last one.'

'But surely that was some time ago?'

'Yes, but it changed me. Changed me for good.'

'I never thought of you as the maternal type.'

'Neither did I. I didn't really want children. But something strange had taken place. I knew I wouldn't ever be the same again. And I didn't want to make love. Can you imagine that?'

'With difficulty.'

'When a woman no longer has any interest in sex she's finished. I came to see the whole thing as ridiculous. It ruined my marriage, of course. I simply wanted to be on my own.'

'And yet you'd been happy?'

'We got along. He wasn't the love of my life. But we both loved the house, our life in France. It's not the same without him.'

The waiter hovered. 'Are you ready to order, sir?'

'Sarah? The grilled sole, I remember, is good.'

'Oh, anything. Sole, yes. No wine for me.'

'And now?'

'I manage.'

'Money?'

'Oh, I'm not poor, if that's what you mean. Neither are you, I take it. You look very much the same as you used to. I don't, I know. No, don't say anything. I know what you're thinking.'

He was in fact appalled by the change in her. The vibrant woman he had known, and as she still was in his memory, was visibly tired, almost defeated. What was almost as bad as her indifference was her seeming inability to rise to the occasion, to do her womanly best to engage with him, ask him the odd question about himself, as he so longed for her to do, if only to rekindle their old exchanges. He missed the scornfulness he was used to. He was obliged to concede that she had changed, almost out of recognition. And the cause, he thought, was not entirely due to illness, but to something less material, less easy to contemplate: the irruption of memory, the fact of ageing, the comparison she was forced to draw between then and now, as if a line had been drawn through her life, facing her with evidence which she was quite unable to accept. Whereas in his own case he had so far managed to disregard such evidence, she was clearly marked by it, and was not to be comforted.

'I'm sorry,' he said, laying aside his napkin. 'I had no idea.'

'Why should you have? You're a man.'

'I'm not going to be put in the wrong just because I'm a man. I remember you so well. The love of my life. What a bore I must have been.'

She smiled. 'We won't go into that again. We both knew where we stood. And now it's all over. Like everything else.'

'Oh, Sarah, please don't say that. We have to go on living, whether we like it or not. All friendships are precious. We relinquish them at our peril. We need one another. At least, I need to know that you are still in my life. It's not easy for me to say this. I dare say I'm just as boring now as you say I was then. My life is boring, I have to admit. And it's easy to lose heart. Enormous effort is required . . .'

'I know what you're saying. I'm sorry if I've let you down.'

'You're here, that's all that matters. The bill, please,' he said, in a voice which to his surprise was quite composed. 'Perhaps this was rather too much my idea. Possibly a mistake.'

'Not entirely. You were always reassuring. And it is remarkable how little you've changed. How have you managed that?'

He sighed. 'I was never very good at change. I am a dull man, with all the characteristics of dullness. Patience, conscientiousness – that sort of thing. I lack – well, whatever it takes to make a success of life. I'm not discontented, well, not entirely. But I know my life lacks all the essentials. You don't want to hear this. That's right,' he said to the waiter.

'Thank you, sir.'

'Come, I'll take you home. But Sarah, do try to do without the stick.'

'If you'll give me your arm . . .'

'Always.'

They walked in silence, unwilling to let each other go, until, with a sigh, he hailed a taxi.

'When will you go to France?'

'Probably at Easter. You're more than welcome to visit me. I'll stay for a few months, maybe longer. And it would be good to see you. I get quite depressed sometimes. I never used to.'

'That's why it's so important not to lose sight of ourselves. What we were. What we are now, though that's more difficult. I don't want to lose you.'

'Even as I am now?'

'Even as you are now. We've both changed. I'm a bore, and you – well, I sometimes thought you had no heart. Now I can see that you were much braver than I was. I suppose I must still love you.'

She squeezed his hand. 'There's a taxi. I'll be perfectly all right.'

'Well, if you're sure. I think I might walk a bit. I'll be in touch. Let me know if you need anything.'

But this somehow was too hearty, too practical. And he was anxious now to be alone. Without her he could think more clearly, more philosophically, could think himself back into his natural solitude. He waved until the taxi was out of sight and then set out to walk home, despite the wind that had sprung up, and the drops of rain that promised a wet afternoon. The weather seemed entirely appropriate. Without forethought, perhaps without any thought at all, they had ventured on to dangerous territory. The facts were unavoidable: she was no longer desirable, and he had never overcome his initial disadvantages. And that they were old, and that this condition was irremediable. His rallying remarks to her had fallen on deaf ears, as they deserved to. In this she was more clear-sighted than he was, and, as ever, unsparing. He thought that they had come closer, she having revealed a pessimism she had not shown previously. And what she said was true: she gave off an aura of fatalism, whereas in the past she had never hesitated to take the initiative. By the same token, his moods of exasperation, though welcome, had made him less acceptable as a companion. For example, he had not seen her to her door, a solecism that was surely out of character, and one he knew that he would actively regret. He was less receptive to the demands of any occasion, just as he was less receptive to other phenomena, works of art being a case in point. He was intolerant of artifice: only a meaningful transparency would do. In that sense their conversation had been a limited success, if a failure in every other respect.

By the time he reached Hyde Park Corner rain was falling steadily, the icy rain of early spring. Waking each morning in the bleak light and gazing round his small bedroom he was filled with a longing for the sun, for which he felt he had waited too long. Getting up, preparing for the day, he felt nothing but resignation. Even this morning, with the prospect of seeing Sarah, there had been no lightening of his mood. He had not actively missed her, or even very much looked forward to seeing her. She awakened demeaning truths. Nor did he welcome her no less demeaning confessions. There should be an embargo on the sort of conversation they had just had. The desire for transparency was not always rewarded. And he had been aware of the changes in her. It was as if she no longer cared for his opinion, or about the opinion of any man. What persisted was the feeling each might have had for an old friend, one known since childhood, fixed in the memory. He supposed that he would visit her in France, if the invitation were to be repeated, but for the time being he would, he knew, be better off on his own, or in the company of those strangers who were the unwitting inhabitants of his everyday life.

For the moment, however, there were more practical considerations. He was wet; rain trickled down from his hair into his collar. There was comfort of a sort in the prospect of getting home, of changing his clothes, of settling in for the rest of the day. He had the beginnings of a headache, one of the severe headaches that had affected him in his youth and from which he had been free for some time. It was a day for invalidism, for cosseting. He would ring Sarah that evening, to excuse himself for what he felt was his failure, or perhaps the failure of his invitation, but in reality had no great wish to speak to her.

Dry, warm, and changed into an old pullover, he went to the window and leaned his head against the glass in an attempt to soothe the dull ache, but also to look for signs of life. To his horror he was rewarded with the sight of Mrs Gardner turning the corner and coming towards him, saw too that she had seen his figure at the window. She waved, with every sign of enthusiasm. Resignedly he waved back. Clearly it was to be his day for female company.

'What a bit of luck,' she said, discarding her scarf. 'Are you making a cup of tea? I'm not interrupting anything, am I?'

In the kitchen he reflected that this was the first and only question she had ever asked him.

'No, you're not interrupting anything,' he said, returning with the tray. 'But I'm afraid I've got a bit of a headache. And I don't seem to have any aspirin. I'll have to go to the chemist.'

'I usually have some in my bag. Here, take a couple of these.'

He was absurdly grateful for this token of consideration, unusual as it was. In fact he felt a sort of gratitude towards her for behaving so normally. As ever she seemed quite accustomed to his undemanding presence, seemed to regard him as someone with an answer to her problems, though those problems did not seem to disturb her.

'How are you finding the flat?' he asked. 'Quite comfortable?'

'Oh, it's ghastly.' She seemed quite cheerful.

'I always thought it rather pleasant, when I used to visit my cousin there. So much bigger than here.'

'Well, if you liked it so much why don't we just change places? You could go there and I could stay here.' At his look of horror she laughed. 'Only joking.'

'I hope so.'

'Well, as you know, I'm looking for some sort of work in town, and it is a bit of a drag coming all this way.'

'And how is that going?'

'Well, I've several irons in the fire. And I'm seeing a solicitor about my financial position. At the moment I'm living on handouts.'

'You've still got your allowance?'

'Oh, yes, but as I explained . . .'

'Yes, yes. But a solicitor's fees might prove more expensive than you realize.'

'He's a friend. I don't suppose it'll cost me anything.'

'Well, you know best.'

He was anxious for her to go, to leave him on his own. Strange how ingrained the habit of solitude had become. Now he longed for the privacy of his own tiny space: even the usual bad news on the radio would be preferable to these increasingly tiresome women. And he doubted if she had been entirely flippant when suggesting that they exchange flats. Even her lightest remarks revealed a certain steeliness of purpose. He wondered what her husband might be thinking of her now. In any event she was her husband's problem. Though in fact she did not appear to see herself as a problem to anyone.

'Headache gone?' she enquired sunnily. 'Well, I suppose I'd better be on my way.' She heaved a theatrical sigh. 'And such a long way. Well, if you have further thoughts . . .'

'Unlikely.'

There was no change in her expression. Yet again he felt a reluctant admiration. She looked at him, apparently without calculation. When she left he could feel the weight of her calculation as he took stock of the flat and saw it with her eyes.

19

This exchange, and the prospect of further exchanges to come – for he did not doubt her pertinacity – activated the concept of home, that great good place to which he had never come and for which he had always yearned. That was the point of those early reminiscences with which he was so familiar. Not that that early home had been satisfactory, rather the opposite. He had exchanged it thankfully for this small anonymous flat and in doing so had thought himself free of uncomfortable associations. Now he realized that a home without associations was not a home at all. He had thought of his flat as the first step towards a better life, one which he would be happy to identify as his own, to which he would invite friends, and, ideally, one which would come with all the attributes of family life. Instead of which his flat remained a temporary refuge, and nothing more. There was nothing to stop him finding somewhere else, but the idea was rebarbative, and in truth another place would pose the same problems. He was forced to concede that his present flat would suit Mrs Gardner's requirements very well, although those requirements proved nebulous. She looked for favours and saw no reason why these should not be offered. She seemed to have had no difficulty in finding temporary shelters, simply because her own needs came first. This inestimable gift annihilated any possible objections, and had almost done so in his case. Only a primitive sense of possession on his part had stood in her way, and this he would not relinquish without a struggle. But it was a struggle for which he had no taste.

Of the two women he had to admit that Mrs Gardner was the more entertaining. Her determination not to be fully questioned was all of a piece with her sense of freedom, a sense which usually evaporates as one reaches the age of maturity. This she had somehow retained. On first encountering her on the plane to Venice he had thought her agreeable, no more, an ordinary woman on her way to friends, whose way of life appeared normal. In time, however, those friends had multiplied, and although anonymous, were somehow omnipresent. Her evasiveness was a way of exculpating herself from obligation: it was pre-emptive, in the sense that it proclaimed her to be guilt free. And it was a technique that seemed to serve her well. She would pay for her company with the endless fascination of seeing her will at work. At least that had been his own reaction. Her lack of curiosity he saw as armour against the world's incursions. Although he strongly disapproved of her he did not question her quality as a life force, a prime mover. Why else had he stood up so urgently outside Florian's in an effort to waylay her, as if he had instinctively understood her purposefulness and had desired to capture some of it for himself?

As for his poor Sarah, he feared she was a lost cause. He knew little of women's illnesses and had no reason to doubt her explanation of her present condition. But there was something about that condition that struck him as unworthy. The woman he had once known would have scorned pathos, would have shuddered at any mention of bodily ills, of pathology. The scorn was still there but it was inconsistent, just enough to remind him, uncomfortably, of the past. Yet he was unable to dismiss the change in her, had to reject any sympathy he might have felt for any other woman in the same situation. He did not wish to know of the stratagems she employed to get her through the day, recognized that these might be arduous, even unattractive. In comparison with her glum realism Mrs Gardner's lack of complexity shone forth in all its lustre, as it had done in their brief meeting in Venice. It was only since their first encounter that he had become aware of a mindset far less transparent than that of Sarah, whom he still knew as he had once known, despite her unbecoming metamorphosis.

And he had looked to one or other of these women to save him from himself! That this was an illusion, and no doubt a fantasy, was quite clear to him. And yet the longing remained, and even the pattern of thought which was somehow indelible: the ideal home, the ideal company. There was the related question of why either of them would want him. Women no longer looked for a husband as they had in the old days; they were now too busy asserting their independence. He sighed with irritation as he read his newspapers in the morning, with their tales of cash settlements for divorcees, or the problems inherent in having it all. Women were no longer beholden: a relationship was just that, a relationship. And yet he knew that both Sarah and Mrs Gardner were needy. The trouble was that the ideology with which they were both familiar forbade any acknowledgement of that need. Of course their needs were very different. Mrs Gardner's needs were temporal and inconclusive; she would always want more, or perhaps something else. Sarah's needs were more difficult to identify. She gave the impression of being ultimately disappointed, unfulfilled. Neither seemed to regret the absence of children, though, he realized, he still did. Yet the sort of family life he desired met no echo in either of them.

What Sarah wanted, of course, and had always wanted, was a man of her own class, more elevated than his own. This was, and always had been, uncomfortable. With his suburban background and essentially suburban tastes he had been found wanting. That had been his own failing, his character being a minor matter. He had chosen to ignore this unstated problem, but the knowledge had existed on both sides, and perhaps still did. What had shown itself as scorn was class confidence, his inability to share it a relic of his undistinguished origins. This matter had never been discussed, though it somehow continued to exist independently, as a given. Only now, with more serious matters to consider, had it been laid to rest. Laid to rest, but not eradicated.

His best companion, he thought, might be a young child, whom he could instruct in the ways of the world but also in the rules of good behaviour. This child would be a boy, perhaps as young as four years of age, and they would take ruminative walks together, observing works of nature such as beetles and squirrels. Any love he felt could be safely invested in such a child, from whom he would desire nothing in return. They would be innocent together, surely an ideal. But no child was available, and he was left with adults and their tedious agendas, their discontent, their fears. His own fears were left unexamined by those putative partners, whose lack of curiosity now struck him as abnormal. In the course of his increasingly troubled nights he longed for purely corporeal comfort from whatever source. Thus his dilemma was without a solution, whether to retain the illusion of perfect innocence, or to seek the alternative illusion, an inevitable compromise, of a makeshift partnership.

He reflected ruefully how little he had changed, how little one does change without an agency to reflect one back at oneself. The only cordiality, the only conviviality he had ever enjoyed had been at work, among men with whom he could at least exchange the day's news. That his colleagues had proved an ersatz form of company mattered little. They had filled a purpose. Even catching the bus in the morning had released him from the solitude of his flat; even the cup of coffee in the café near the bank had cheered him. It was in that café that he had made his first contact with those strangers who he thought would stand him in good stead, if, like Stendhal, he were to collapse in the street. This had not yet happened, but his reflex was to look around him in order to arm himself against such an eventuality. The reflex was still in place: he still left the flat in the morning with a feeling of deliverance; he still maintained a reduced form of cordiality with people he did not know. When he reflected on these matters the desire for change was uppermost in his mind. How to bring this about was still unclear, the choices available to him pitifully small. Yet change he must, even if it meant marrying a woman with whom he was slightly at odds. And even if he made a bad choice he would enjoy the luxury of conformity, of joining the majority. He had no doubt that he would be able to play his part; conformity was in his nature. He saw this not as a weakness, but, on the contrary, as a strength, even a recommendation. He looked forward keenly to becoming a member of that hearty incurious crowd among whose customs he had sought a form of validation, of acceptance.

The only dignified alternative to these markedly undignified calculations was some form of exile. That at least would have the advantage of prestige. He would be the resident Englishman abroad, like Somerset Maugham or Graham Greene, though without their accomplishments. This scenario had much to recommend it. He could live in an hotel – always the hotel – and spend his days sitting in the sun until the money ran out. Then, of course, he would have to come home, although in such a context the word 'home' would have lost its baleful associations. Death would follow in due course, always with the hope of an attendant, known or unknown. Try as he might he could not see either Sarah or

Mrs Gardner in this role. Nor could he expect them to be present if he had deserted them during his sojourn abroad. All things considered he might do better to remain in touch, and if that meant living out his days in London then that would be the price to be paid. His current loneliness would be abandoned somehow, though the choices before him remained unattractive.

There remained the immediate problem of Mrs Gardner's desire to move into his flat, or rather to send him off to Helena's flat where he had no desire to be. She would do this by the simple expedient of turning up again with her luggage, and he could think of no good reason why he should object to this. Her own arguments would suffice: that it would be a purely temporary measure until her husband came up with enough money to enable her to acquire some place of her own. But why should she bother to do this if already comfortably lodged in his own flat? In any event her comings and goings were a matter which she managed not to clarify, and this obfuscation remained a considerable obstacle in his dealings with her. And would continue to do so. He even wondered if her husband knew where she was, though she had every reason to keep in touch with him, predominantly through the solicitor friend who, she claimed, would give his services free of charge. He did not doubt this either. She was an attractive woman, and, by present standards, she had a case for compensation. And she needed an address from which to operate. He could not help but remember their lunch in Venice, when he had asked her whether she still loved her husband. Yes, she had said, and her expression had been one of distant nostalgia. That expression had disappeared, to be replaced by one of complete opacity. And who could blame her? She was under no obligation to reveal any secret longings she might have harboured. Nevertheless he locked up carefully as he prepared to leave his flat. He even wondered whether to have a word with the caretaker, until he reproached himself for such idiociy. This, however, was yet another reminder that he had been alone for far too long.

The fact that he continued to think of her as Mrs Gardner while addressing her as Vicky was significant perhaps, though what it signified was not quite clear. It was indicative, he thought, of her sheer otherness, which remained her most potent attraction, in comparison with which Sarah's attitude of slightly condescending compliance was less endearing. But they had a history, Sarah and he, and not merely their own. They went back in time, remembered the same things. They were, in terms of age, travelling the same route. More to the point, he could not imagine his life without her, whether or not love came into it. In fact love was by this stage somewhat superfluous, in the sense that it had taken place already. There was no need to go down that road again.

Such speculations were unsettling. He decided that what he needed was a long walk, preferably away from the working world which now felt like a reproach. He would cross the park and make his way back via the Albert Hall. His property, such as it was, must be left to fate. He had a strong desire to renounce all responsibility. Responsibility had been his lot for as long as he could remember.

The telephone rang as he was putting on his coat. It occurred to him that he need not answer it, but the habit was too strong.

'It's Sarah. Just to thank you for lunch. You were right, the food was excellent.'

'I'm afraid I . . .'

'What I wanted to say was that I've decided to go to the house for a few days. Just to check up.'

'How long will you be away?'

'Only a few days. I'll go down for a longer spell after Easter. Did I say that?'

'You did, yes.'

'My memory is not what it was. Getting older.'

'Oh, come, Sarah. You seem determined to think yourself into old age. That stick, for instance.'

'You seem to manage pretty well. How do you do it?'

'I don't *do* anything.'

'You're a good deal sharper than you used to be.'

He was shocked. 'Sharper?'

'Critical.'

'Well, I'll defend my right to be critical. Actually I felt badly about not seeing you home. I wanted to walk a bit, and I didn't particularly want to go home.'

'That flat . . .'

'As you say, that flat. And yet they tell me that these flats are hotly contested. I get enquiries. I had one yesterday.'

But this was dangerous territory. In any event such lines were not to be crossed.

'If I sound ratty it's probably the effect of living alone for so long.'

'Yes, I know about that. Do you ever think we might have . . .'

'Oh, no, not really. You were too cautious for me. I wanted more adventure in my life. Funny how we met up again.'

'Only to realize how much time had passed.'

There was a pause.

'Let's not have this conversation again. It does neither of us any favours.'

There was a short silence while they digested his remark.

'When do you leave for France?'

'Next Monday. So don't worry if you ring and don't get an answer.'

'When do I see you again?'

'Another lunch?'

'Why not?'

'I should be back after a week or ten days.'

'I'll telephone.'

'If you say so.'

He rang off, dissatisfied. Was it his own age, old by any standards, that accounted for this discomfiture, this reluctance, this searching for a remedy? He longed for a cure for this non-existent illness but very real malady. Was desire really dead, leaving in its wake mere fantasy? Was he deluded into thinking he had a choice? It was in a desire to beat the odds that he seized his hat and strode out, determined to prove to any witnesses that he was still capable of independent progress. Any doubts that surfaced would be – must be – robustly denied.

20

In the interests of ownership he decided to go to Helena's flat with a view to putting it on the market. This, he reckoned, would finance his sojourn on the shores of the Mediterranean, which, with the onset of lighter mornings, now began to look more plausible, more pleasurable. Although still cold the weather held promise of warmer days to come, yet he was suddenly too impatient to sit out the inevitable slow improvement. In the mornings he could hear pigeons: their mournful notes seemed redolent of England and its slowness, which infected his every movement, his lack of decisiveness. In the sun he would regain some of his early vigour, would be entitled to abandon his conscientious comings and goings down familiar streets, and by the same token to abandon the one fantasy which had preoccupied him and which he now saw was unlikely to be substantiated. At a stroke he would rid himself of ties which were becoming problematic, if not onerous. How this was to be done he was unsure; he only knew that if he got rid of Mrs Gardner he could reassert his autonomy in some way, put an end to speculation, both hers and his own, and make a free choice, if such a thing were ever possible, about the future. It suddenly seemed a matter of urgency to do this; his birthday had brought in its wake a new sense that he was old, that there was little time left before incapacity claimed him. He was still able, but he knew that this would not last, and although reassuring when Sarah complained of her poor health he was not unaware of those fears, those warnings, when it came to his own life. Indeed his words of comfort to her might soon be applied to himself, and he viewed with extreme distaste the exchange of symptoms that might be their lot. Besides, getting rid of Helena's flat would be tantamount to getting rid of the entanglement that Mrs Gardner had brought in her wake. He had no desire to encourage further fantasies on her part, or indeed on his own.

Yet the distance travelled between his own small flat and the looming red brick structure he had known mostly from dark evenings after his visits to Helena infected him with an unwelcome melancholy which he thought he had banished. His memory of that relationship was equally dark, her un-doubted stoicism striking him anew as not admirable but pitiable. Even in daylight, on a relatively bright morning, the building seemed minatory, untenanted. There was no sound from behind the closed doors; his feet made silent progress in the thickly carpeted corridors; no face met his own on the stairs. Inside the flat the noiselessness was compounded by absence. He moved to the nearest window for a sign of outdoor life, but all he could see was a bus stop at which nobody waited. In almost total silence he longed for the sound of a footfall or the sight of a pedestrian, but neither sight nor sound presented itself. This sensory absence convinced him yet again that he could never live here, nor indeed could Mrs Gardner, on whose behalf he felt a renewal of sympathy. No woman could be assigned to this place without undergoing the same isolation that had afflicted Helena. He saw that his acts of good will, towards both Helena and Mrs Gardner, had been interpreted as something of an insult, an act of charity which both had rejected with hauteur. He felt a renewed distaste for his own calculations.

As he inspected the rooms the silence became even more palpable. There was no sign of occupancy apart from the unmade bed, with the inevitable bags left where he had last seen them. In the kitchen two cups and saucers, unwashed, stood on the draining board. Had she, even here, found company? Or, more likely, did she leave them for someone else to take care of? He was momentarily touched by the frail old-fashioned cups: his mother had possessed such a tea service, of a kind common in the thirties used for visitors, and as much a sign of gentility as polished shoes and a matching handbag. All this belonged to the past, as did that same silk dressing-gown he had brought home from the hospital and which now trailed on the floor. He picked it up and laid it on the bed: he would not go so far as to open the doors of cupboards, as if fearful of what their contents would reveal, either of absence or of presence. He was emphatically out of place.

The sitting-room was unchanged, apart from a further cup and saucer, equally unwashed, on the bookcase. He retrieved the copy of *Emma* which had been opened and placed face down on the table, and for a moment stood wondering what to do with it. Clearly Mrs Gardner had sought momentary solace in Jane Austen and then relinquished her support. He could not blame her: there was little point of contact between them. He wondered where she was, though this was a fruitless speculation. He would leave a note for her, requesting a phone call. He would, he decided, lose no time in putting this flat on the market. He would definitely not want to see it again.

He took a last look round, one part of him registering the desirability of such a property in the current market, while rejecting any feeling of ownership on his own behalf. He acknowledged that the rooms were more spacious than those in his own flat, but that the atmosphere was curiously confining. Whereas he had no trouble in leaving his own flat in the mornings (was indeed in a hurry to do so), he would find it difficult to extricate himself from these mournful spaces, might indeed sit here all day, awaiting some spectral visitor such as himself. He remembered his dream of the flat with the missing window which had so alarmed him, and realized that the dream was simply a mask for the reality of those Sunday visits, of these very rooms. He made a final inspection. Only the bathroom yielded a sign of occupancy: two towels left on the floor, and an almost empty tube of toothpaste on the side of the washbasin. As he turned to leave he noticed a used tea bag on the rim of the bath.

He left as silently as he had entered. Although longing to lock the door he left it as Mrs Gardner had left it and went in search of the caretaker. Only another man, he felt, could enlighten him as to her movements. But there was no one in the basement. Rather than prolong the process, and with no desire to go back inside the flat, he went in search of coffee, in as crowded a place as he could find. He was now possessed of an urgent desire to settle this matter as soon as possible, as if time were of the essence, or rather to annihilate the spectre of time passing before he could be free of the place. The sun, he thought, the sun, as if he were a benighted pagan, fearful of all dark places, of night, of winter, of every form of abandonment.

After the unearthly quiet of the flat street life struck him as almost exotic. He found a café and sat down with relief, regretting that he had not brought his newspaper with him. The coffee was good, stronger, it seemed, than the sort he would have drunk close to home, the sort of coffee that would have appealed to European exiles, if these still existed. He had no obligation either to linger or to hurry, yet the task awaiting him seemed fraught with urgency, if only the urgency of putting the matter behind him once and for all. Mrs Gardner would have to be contacted, of course, and that, he hoped, would be the end of her. At least it would be the end of his responsibility towards her. What came next must be a matter of free will, his no less than hers.

On his return he found the caretaker sweeping the front steps. 'Good morning,' he said. 'I don't know if you remember me. Sturgis is my name. I am now the owner of the late Mrs Sturgis's flat. I should have explained that I've lent it to a friend, but I doubt if she'll be staying. It's Mr . . . ?'

'Call me Arthur. That's what they all call me, all the residents, that is. I've been here too long. Well, that'll all change in a few months when I retire. I doubt if they'll replace me. Not at this salary, at any rate. If you'd like to come in.'

'I won't take up much of your time . . .'

'To be honest I'm glad you've turned up. I didn't like what I heard from that flat, footsteps and so on. Then it all went quiet. Seems there's nobody there now. But you can't leave property empty these days, not even in this area. Vandals. Joyriders. Know what I mean?'

'I'll see to that. I shan't be living there myself. I'll probably sell it in the very near future. I'll leave you my telephone number, er, Arthur, and let you know my plans as soon as I know them myself. I may be going abroad,' he added, although the prospect once again struck him as fanciful. That, of course, was the price to pay for solitary decisions which involved no one but oneself. But this put him back in the realm of speculation, and what he needed now were firm decisions, preferably hard-headed and as realistic as possible.

'You'll get a good price if you decide to sell,' the man said. 'I was going to make myself a cup of tea.'

'I won't detain you.'

'Only I could get you a new owner, no problem. I've had enquiries. Save you going through an agency. Know what I mean?'

'Of course. I'd be very grateful. We can discuss this when . . .'

'If you'd like to join me in a cup of tea we could discuss the matter of price. And I'll need to know how to contact you.'

'I'll give you both my numbers,' he said, following the man to his flat in the basement. 'Oh, how much lighter it seems down here. And how nice you've made it.'

It did indeed seem attractive, mainly with signs of occupancy, two chairs and a small table in what was clearly a much lived in kitchen, a kettle already filled and waiting. Meekly he sat down. This man obviously considered him an equal in the matter of buying and selling, though there was no doubt which of them occupied a more advantageous position.

'Yes, well, the wife does all that. Not that we won't be glad to see the back of it. We've got a little place in Essex, lovely it is. That's why I'm looking forward to retirement. So if we could come to some arrangement as soon as possible . . .'

'Of course. I'll be in touch as soon as I can.'

He endured a lengthy recital of the amenities of the house in Essex, the en-suite bathrooms, the patio doors, the state-of-the-art sound system, before standing up to leave. 'I'll be in touch,' he repeated.

'If you want to remove any personal possessions I'd do it now if I were you.'

But this was taking entrepreneurship a little too far. Further pleasantries were exchanged, and then, finally, he was free to go.

It occured to him to wonder how and when such monies were to be conveyed, and also the crucial matter of how much commission was expected. A hundred pounds? Five hundred? To be on the safe side he opted for five hundred, assuming that this was the going rate. He had no knowledge of such transactions, having never been in receipt of financial favours and being rigorously correct in such matters. He surmised that the house in Essex had profited from Arthur's commission. Perhaps he had been expected to hand over money straight away, as a pledge of good faith, but the banker in him objected to such unsupervised disbursements. The transaction would, of course, never be referred to, an envelope discreetly handed over, or left on that kitchen table. Five hundred, he decided, and that would be the end of it. How and when he decided to leave was unclear. He would be relieved of the flat, need never see it again. For five hundred pounds it would be disposed of sight unseen.

There remained the problem of how to convey this news to Mrs Gardner, or rather the intractable problem of Mrs Gardner herself. A pragmatist might have solved it by going to live with her in the flat, and being the conventional man he longed to be. But this was deeply unattractive. He had left a note asking her to telephone but doubted that she would, her preferred method of communication being to call on him unannounced. There was the further problem of getting her to leave, although she professed to loathe the place, much as he had come to do. She remained something of a menace, with her seemingly eternal rootlessness, but there was no need for him to assume responsibility for her movements. That he continued to do so was merely a sign of his own weakness. Those other friends, who would be expected to accommodate her, might in fact feel as reluctant as he now did. And his own small flat was in her sights, and had been, he now realized, as soon as she had first entered it.

It was a relief to be out in the air, away from the business of property, his own or anyone else's. It was only out in the air that he felt untrammelled, in command of himself. That was probably the reason why he took so many walks, not, as he thought, because he was simply hungry for faces. Air was his element, weightlessness his ideal condition. There was little chance that this would continue indefinitely. He was in his seventy-fourth year, still in relatively good health, but apt to tire abruptly, like a small child. He had only his will to see him through, and that must not be surrendered. Therefore all depredations must be resisted, even if the effort were to be, or to seem, disproportionate. He had a strong desire for a solution that he would not have to engineer for himself. He did not doubt that this was a common wish, a willed helplessness of which he could not approve, long for it though he might. He was a grown man, he reminded himself: he must see it through. At the same time he regretted that he could rely only on himself. But that too was a common wish, inappropriate in an adult. Except that others seemed to bring it off, Mrs Gardner being a case in point.

The air revived him. He breathed deeply, newly indifferent to others. Every step he took seemed to armour him against further incursions. He would have liked to discuss matters with someone, Sarah being the obvious choice. She would have regarded him with astonishment, laughed at his scruples, reproached him as she had always done, launched into her usual barrage of criticisms. For once he would have welcomed all this. But Sarah was out of town, and he wanted the matter settled as soon as possible. Unfortunately Mrs Gardner was also out of touch and likely to remain so until she chose to re-enter his orbit. He saw all too clearly why he had failed with women. It was his desire to see them in a good light that had let him down. Even when they were manifestly at fault he had withheld his reproaches. There had been those who simply drifted away, baffled by his restraint. This too, he thought, was a matter of class, his own politeness having been drilled into him by parents too anxious not to give offence. He had never been able to overcome this predisposition, could not see it as a virtue. Only someone known from infancy might have seen it that way. But the days of innocence were long gone. Against his expectations the age of reason was proving something of a disappointment.

21

His reading now was confined to diaries, notebooks, memoirs, anything that contained a confessional element. He was in search of evidence of discomfiture, disappointment, rather than triumph, over circumstances. Circumstances, he knew, would always overrule. Those great exemplars of the past, the kind he had always sought in classic novels, usually finished on a note of success, of exoneration, which was not for him. In the absence of comfort he was forced to contemplate his own failure, failure not in worldly terms but in the reality of his circumscribed life. He knew, rather more clearly than he had ever known before, that he had succeeded only at mundane tasks, that he had failed to deliver a reputation that others would acknowledge. Proof, if proof were needed, lay in the fact that his presence was no longer sought, that, deprived of the structure of the working day, he was at a loss, obliged to look for comfort in whatever he could devise for himself. His life of reading, of walking, was invisible to others: his friendships, so agreeable in past days, had dwindled, almost disappeared. Memories were of no use to him; indeed, even memory was beginning to be eroded by the absence of confirmation. As to love, that was gone for good. Whatever he managed to contrive for himself would not, could not, be construed as success.

Sarah was absent, and their last meeting had, he saw, pleased neither of them. Each mirrored the unwelcome changes in the other. To all intents and purposes sympathetic, he had merely been spruce and jocular, attitudes unlikely to appeal to any woman once known intimately. She had a past of which he knew too little, merely the outlines: a husband now relegated to some sort of prehistory, a house in France to which she resorted from time to time, a life lived without enthusiasm. This differed from the life that had so fascinated him during the years when he had been in thrall to her decisiveness, even when that decisiveness excluded him. Now she saw him only as a relic of her own refulgent past, and one that was not flattering. He was dismayed by the changes in her, which, he knew, afflicted her in ways with which she was not familiar. Illness, infirmity, whether real or imagined, were a cover for a distress very different from her old impatience. They would meet from time to time, but any pleasure would soon turn to irony, as if re-enactment of a ritual were a worthy substitute for what had once been meaningful. The saving grace, if grace it could be called, was that they both knew this and had decided that it was better than nothing. And though he could not answer for her in this or any other matter, he thought that she felt the same. Thus their defeat united them in ways which neither of them entirely welcomed. Circumstances again. What had once been their youth was now something of a myth: the cruelty of age now constituted a common ground which he found easier to tolerate than Sarah evidently did. His training in obscurity, in duty conscientiously performed, but performed without *réclame*, had resulted in a sense of endurance in which he took no pride. For a woman, he knew, or thought he knew, this would be even worse. Sarah's pride had always resided in her success with men, her unshakeable confidence that she could command their feelings for her, that she would always have a choice. Now she had even less of a choice than he had. Only the memory of attachment remained, that and certain moments of affection, when she took his arm, leaned against him. But then went back to whatever life she lived now, one for which she obviously had little taste. His own desire for disclosure, for total knowledge of the other, of others, remained unfulfilled.

As for Mrs Gardner, he was even more at a loss, though a loss that contained an intriguing element of mystery. His sympathy, which had once been aroused, had fallen into abeyance, and yet the very irritation he felt was something of a stimulus. He wanted her out of his way, and yet he wanted to follow her story. He remembered her saying that she felt lucky, that she was being looked after by some benign providence; he had thought this absurd, but had not had the heart to tell her so. But perhaps that was all it took, a willingness to assume that all would be well. That willingness extended even to himself: he would accede to her wishes, or at least she assumed that he would, under the benign gaze of that entity to which she entrusted her fate. And if her wishes were not immediately fulfilled she would not take it amiss, would simply present them from time to time, as she no doubt had when she contacted her husband, or ex-husband. There was matter here for comedy rather than for tragedy: that was the essence of her attraction. The trouble was that those who believed in their own destiny usually proved something of a burden for others. He could only count on her presence, or absence – absence on the whole being preferable – for as long as she decreed, his own will in the matter defeated by her curious blitheness, for which his admiration remained undimmed.

Momentarily rendered philosophical by these reflections, he was almost annoyed when the telephone rang. He was not ready to contemplate further action, at least not at that moment. He decided to be prime mover in any action that was to be taken, to assert his autonomy in the face of those same circumstances against which he had no protection. There was no need to accede to others' difficulties, sympathize though he surely would. His sympathy, he thought, was, and would remain, a constant.

'Arthur here,' said a voice in his ear.

'Arthur?'

'Your flat. I've got a lady here interested in it. Wants to know how much you want for it.'

He had no idea how much the flat was worth but named a sum which he considered astronomical. There was a muttered conversation, a hand having been placed over the mouthpiece.

'No problem,' came back in a normal tone. 'Lady's name is Mrs Fitch. Says she's going out to lunch but could meet you here this afternoon, if that's convenient.'

'Certainly. Shall we say two-thirty?'

Again the hand was placed over the mouthpiece. 'Two-thirty is fine.' 'Sir,' was added.

Clearly Arthur was the linchpin in these negotiations. Five hundred, he reckoned.

As a guarantee of good faith he went straight to the bank. That he was being out-manoeuvred he had no doubt. But did it matter? He had little feeling for the flat, but spared a thought for Helena, whose province it had been, and whose presence had seemed so palpable on his recent visit. The money was almost irrelevant, was quite unreal. Events seemed to be making up his mind for him: he had not yet decided what to do. Too restless to go home he took a taxi to the flat, anxious now to present himself, as if he, rather than this Mrs Fitch, were the supplicant.

He found Arthur in the basement, making tea. He placed his envelope on the kitchen table without comment. Equally without comment it was removed to a drawer. He was offered, and accepted, a cup of tea.

'That was quick,' he said.

'Yes, well, she's enquired a couple of times. I didn't like to

153

say anything when your friend was here, but now she seems to have gone . . . As I say, you can't leave property empty these days.'

'She's coming back at two-thirty, you say?'

'Gone out to lunch with her daughter. It's on account of the daughter that she wants to come back to London. Been living in the country, doesn't know whether to keep the place on there. Not short of a few bob, I should say. Knows what she wants and how to get it.'

So money had been exchanged on her part as well as on his. What further improvements to the house in Essex could now be put in train? Underfloor heating, perhaps. He felt admiration for this man, who also knew what he wanted and how to get it.

'I'll go out and get a bite to eat,' he said. 'Thank you for your help. I'm sure we can wrap things up as soon as we've exchanged the names of our solicitors.'

'Well, you don't want to hang about. I reckon this is her last offer. There's a place round the corner if you want lunch. Though if I was you I'd be back before two-thirty.'

'I have every intention of doing so. To the left or to the right?'

'Left. And much obliged.' 'Sir,' was once again added, not quite as an afterthought. At least he had got that right.

As ever he felt reprieved once he was out in the air, away from property, from proprietorship, from negotiations. The answer to his frequent bouts of distress, he thought, was simply to stay out as long as possible. His strength seemed suddenly in rather short supply. He found the restaurant and sat down heavily, gazing abstractedly at the menu, annoyed at the further decision forced on him. He was not hungry, wanted only coffee, but ordered a dish of pasta, thinking it would supply some much needed energy. Beyond the windows the weather seemed bright, brighter than when he had left home, but cold. In Saint-Paul-de-Vence, where Sarah was, it would be warm. Suddenly he longed for her return. She was his familiar, and by the same token his harshest critic. But even that harshness would be welcome on a day like today, when old associations were being stripped from him. He would, of course, be glad to be rid of the place, was, he supposed, grateful for the promptness with which this had been effected, but would have liked more time in which to think his way forward.

He was back in Arthur's basement by just after two, thinking he had no further right to enter his, or rather Helena's flat, though it was still his. Distantly he wondered how to convey the news to Mrs Gardner, who still had a set of keys. This was a problem he decided to leave to Arthur to sort out. Once dispossessed, and thus restored to her natural condition, she would surely turn up sooner or later. But this was an old problem, and one to which, as ever, there was no solution.

A piercing female voice, accompanied by reassuring noises from Arthur, alerted him to the fact that the business of the day had yet to be completed. He detached himself from the wall against which he had been leaning and stood resolutely awaiting the arrival of Mrs Fitch who, to judge from the timbre of her voice, was as resolute as he was preoccupied. Descending footsteps brought them face to face, with Arthur in attendance. To his surprise Mrs Fitch was elderly, even older than himself, but by no means undermined by this fact. Rather the opposite: she scrutinized him very much as if prepared to find him wanting in some essential way. This, again, was to be a matter of class, he concluded. 'Paul Sturgis,' he announced, holding out his hand. 'Mrs Fitch, I believe?'

'I'm in rather a hurry, I'm afraid. I trust that this won't take long?'

'If you'd give me the name of your solicitor, I'm sure we can exchange quite speedily. I've written down my man's name and address. How soon would you . . . ?'

'As I've said, as soon as possible.' She took the card from his outstretched hand and examined it. 'Quite a reputable firm, I believe. I may even have met this man at some point. Have you been with him long?'

He felt his credentials were in the balance. 'Yes, ever since I retired.'

'There's the matter of clearing the flat. Of course I have my own furniture, some of it rather valuable.' More valuable than poor Helena's, he was given to understand. 'If there's anything you want to take perhaps you'd do so now. My son-in-law will see to transport. Or perhaps you have someone . . .'

'No, I have no one.' The mournful phrase horrified him. 'I live in a small flat, with no room to spare. There's nothing I want from here.'

'You realize that the contents will have to be disposed of?'

'Yes, well, if you have no need of them. I believe everything is as my cousin left it, down to the cups and saucers.'

There was an almost audible sniff. 'Hardly to my taste, I'm afraid. In fact it would help if you could dispose of them. Or indeed take them away with you, if you came by car.'

'I did not come by car, and I must leave the matter to you. Or to Arthur, who has been exceedingly helpful.'

'No problem,' said Arthur, who had missed nothing of this exchange.

'In that case, Mr . . . I'm afraid I'm hopeless with names.'

'Sturgis,' he said, his patience suddenly evaporating. 'If you'd like to take another look I'll leave you with Arthur. I have one or two things to see to.' This was untrue. 'I'll look in again before I go home.' This was for Arthur's benefit, rather than hers. He was anxious to get away from the sound of her voice. Further discussion would, he saw, be useless. Besides, he was indignant on Helena's behalf, her cups and saucers spurned, and with them her taste. If interests were to be identified he would unhesitatingly spring to Helena's defence, and to the defence of everything she stood for, pretentious though that had been. Social anxiety may have been her lot too, valiantly disguised though it had been. Her cups and saucers may have been the only relic of her earlier life, before he knew her. He saw nothing amiss with her taste, indeed saw it as entirely respectable, over-stuffed sofas included. He was to be at the mercy, it seemed, of intractable women. It was just that some were less agreeable than others.

He took a pointless walk round the neighbourhood, in order to dissipate his very real antagonism to this woman. The surroundings were no more to his taste than before, but the streets seemed relatively innocent compared with the machinations involved in disposing of his property. He had no desire to see Mrs Fitch again, but supposed he had some sort of duty to Arthur, who had engineered the whole project. He wanted to get back to his own flat, wanted to put this place behind him. He rang the bell to the basement flat and was admitted promptly.

'Cup of tea?'

'No, thank you. I came to say, take whatever you want from the flat. I have no use for any of it.'

'That's very kind of you. Not that we haven't got all our own stuff. Still, some of it might come in handy. Knows what she wants all right, doesn't she? I'll have my work cut out with that one. Do this, do that. Still, I'll be off soon.'

'I envy you. And you've done a good job. I'm very grateful.' A ten-pound note changed hands, and was secreted in a pocket.

'There's just one thing. Thank you, sir. I took the liberty of removing the lady's luggage. Just in case she wonders where it had got to.'

He opened a cupboard and dragged out Mrs Gardner's bags. 'Shall I call you a taxi? They're not heavy, just a bit bulky.'

With despair he possessed himself once again of Mrs Gardner's effects, with despair installed them once again in his bedroom. This, it seemed, was to be his fate. How had it come to this? Six months ago he had been unencumbered, paying his dues, making provision for his own eventual demise. Now he was beset by complications. He would do well to avoid further entanglements. This, however, would not be easy. The looming evidence of the bags in his bedroom seemed to mock his desire to live a boring but peaceful life. As ever, circumstances had got the better of him, as they did of everyone. There was some small, very small, consolation in the fact that he was not alone in this.

22

Now he had more money than he needed, and no one to whom he could leave it. There was no shortage of good causes, but then he would not know how wisely the money was being spent. He remembered Mrs Gardner's references to her work at some Aids charity, and the astonishing amounts of money made available to the victims, or perhaps merely to the administration. This was a problem he could not solve, one of many, the most prominent being his feeling of indignation at Mrs Fitch's prospective despoliation of Helena's effects. He felt this indignation on behalf of all those who had to make their own way up the social ladder, and thus, inevitably, himself.

He could not hide from himself the knowledge that little bound him to Helena's memory apart from those ghostly Sunday afternoon visits in which he acted merely as audience. Yet even these had instilled a measure of respect for a woman who had contrived a life for herself, fictitious though this may have been. His parents, those silent but loyal antagonists, had felt the same respect as soon as she had entered their orbit. They had, not incorrectly, perceived her as superior to themselves, conscious as they were of the failure of their own lives, lives lived joylessly in the knowledge that they had succumbed to the poor choices with which they had been faced, had made a pact with each other not to complain, though knowing that they would have done better with different partners. Of the two his father did his duty, but with grim determination, intent on fulfilling his obligations to the social order. His mother, he now recognized, suffered the same unhappiness that he himself had experienced as a child, the same fretful loneliness. Helena had promised an introduction to a wider world. He remembered her wedding breakfast, the relative sophistication of the attentive waitresses, and the promise of similar celebrations to come. These had not materialized, his parents relegated to some dim limbo to which she had paid little attention. His mother had been tormented by hints that these celebrations were being enjoyed by others, much as he had taken seriously Helena's accounts of activities to which he had no access. He saw now, and perhaps had always suspected, the flimsiness of these impressions, his parents, and perhaps he himself, mistaking this fleeting connection for a semblance of family, having no real family to fill the gap.

Of the two of them his father was the more grimly realistic, making no secret of his disappointment. To his father Sturgis owed his career, although he was conscious of having done rather better in the relative success of his own endeavours, once undergone simply in the hope of winning that same father's approbation. His mother, he realized, had been inconsolable. In truth they were all unhappy. His own unhappiness had been made bearable by thoughts of escape, and this, to his surprise, he had achieved, through his work. Yet what had been bred in him by their silence was the very opposite of their native disposition: a desperate assiduity, a desire to be of service, to prove his good will in every possible circumstance. Too nice, Sarah had judged him, and he had always secretly acknowledged the truth of this, for his niceness was a learned response to indifference rather than genuine inclination. He was thus a failure by his own standards and only by dint of extreme privacy had he kept this hidden from others. In this he had succeeded, but it was a poor success. And it had left him in the same situation as his mother, all those years ago, longing to be included in a family network which she had failed to contrive for herself.

In this context Helena retained her prestige, despite the reality of her widowhood and the solitude that manifested itself in her undisturbed rooms, the stateliness of her pretensions, which he had never bothered to verify, seeing them as her armour, although the artifice prevented either of them from speaking the truth. The truth, their truth, had never been subjected to examination. They had succeeded in maintaining a fiction of kinship, and he did not doubt that she felt as little as he did. Her death had not much affected him: indeed having seen the conditions to which she had been subjected in the hospital he was as glad for her as he would have been for himself in such circumstances. But oddly it was the sight of the flat that had affected him, so obviously bereft of a human presence, so filled with the amenities with which she had ordered her own existence, and so summarily dismissed by the odious Mrs Fitch, for whom he now felt considerable enmity. He would have preferred to leave the flat empty for a while, perhaps a few months, though he knew this was impractical; it would have been a mark of respect, that same respect that his mother must have felt, and that had not been reciprocated.

These memories of the past, unleashed by as little as the sight of those fragile teacups – Proust again – did little to assuage his habitual melancholy. Nor did the realization that with the disappearance of this connection he was now truly free of the past. He would not regret this. In attempting to see himself as others saw him he also saw that he had become the character he thought suitable: appearance had become reality. He was respectable; he had nothing to hide. But having nothing to hide meant an inner emptiness, and a predisposition to any fantasy that might fill that onerous gap. On the face of it there was nothing untoward in his desire, or more accurately his impulse to forge an alliance with a woman, even though the age in which such choices were spontaneous now lay in the distant past. It was this knowledge, the consciousness that time was running out, that made him persist, never quite translating it into reality but seriously entertaining it as a possible strategy. And there was that other fantasy: the escape to the sun, a sun no less physical than metaphysical, the exile in some undemanding place, and the reality of a solitude which had always been his and which he had never managed to overcome.

His cousin Roland was his, and his parents', icon of masculinity, though Roland was to let the side down by dying relatively young. This at least provided a topic of conversation, and the opportunity of a visit of condolence that was the occasion of his first sight of the flat. The death of his father had provoked a return visit; the same thing had happened after his mother's death, and after that the Sunday visits had been inaugurated. When asked how she did, her invariable response was, 'My diary is full.' At first he had taken this at face value. It was only gradually that it dawned on him that this was not entirely true, a fact confirmed by her lonely death in the hospital. But both were slaves to convention and the fiction was loyally maintained. Now she was gone, and with her any remote familial link. He was now free, and rich, as he had once longed to be. But neither the money nor the freedom had brought a sense of ease, rather the opposite. Only the fantasy of choice remained.

Thinking of the past brought him round to Sarah's point of view. It was hateful because it encoded one's mistakes, and was thus less about youth than about what one had done with it, and how close it had brought one to the fact of mortality. For Sarah this was self-evident: she saw herself, or chose to see herself, as impaired, not merely altered but fatally altered. He had brushed aside her fears, but might have done better to take them seriously. If he had not done so it was from fear of contagion. Newly alive to what might constitute a threat, he persisted in routines which had lost their meaning, in an effort to prove to himself that little time had passed between then and now, and that he was in essence unchanged.

He sighed at the prospect of a day alone with his thoughts: the limits of freedom were soon reached. As he left the flat he was not altogether displeased to see Mrs Gardner swinging along the road in his direction, bringing with her evidence of self-sufficiency, of a welcome lack of regret.

'Vicky,' he said. 'Good to see you. I was wondering where you'd got to.'

There was little sign that she was pleased to see him. Indeed she was almost stern, as if she considered him seriously at fault.

'Shall we go in? It's rather cold out here.'

It was indeed cold, the weather having retreated into a greyness, a lack of colour, despite the blossom, the tentative hint of green of reviving nature.

'You've had breakfast?' he queried.

'I could do with a cup of coffee. As you can imagine I can't get into that flat. Not that I'm not glad to see the back of it. What's going on?'

'I had an offer for the place. I told you I intended to sell it. And the buyer was rather insistent. So it's no longer available, I'm afraid.'

'I couldn't care less about the flat. But what about my stuff?'

'Your stuff, as you call it, is here. But not for much longer, Vicky. You really must find another place for it.'

'Easier said than done. I haven't yet got a place of my own.'

'Why don't you go back home?' This sounded so peremptory that he regretted the question as soon as it was put. 'Here, drink your coffee.'

'With another woman there? No, thank you. Anyway, I'm off to New York in a few days. Might as well be there as here. I must say I'm rather surprised at your attitude.'

'But you knew that this was a purely temporary agreement. Or rather no agreement at all.'

'In your place I'd have . . .'

Suddenly he lost patience. 'My dear girl, you can't rely on strangers to help you out.' Though, he realized, that was what he had always done. 'They can't always meet your needs. Why should they? The world is fundamentally indifferent to one's needs.'

'I'm not talking philosophy here. I just know we're on this earth to help one another. That's what I was taught, anyway.'

'Well, your husband . . .'

'Let's not bring him into this discussion. I did go home, if you really want to know. We had a blazing row.' She smiled reminiscently. 'Just like old times. So, no, I can't go there again.'

'New York? You've friends there who can put you up for a while?'

'I've got friends all over the world.'

He remembered her saying this before. 'It would help if you'd leave me a telephone number. I suppose you're going to tell me that you want to leave your bags here. But I don't think you can, Vicky.'

'Why not? It's a small thing to ask.'

'I may be going abroad,' he said desperately. 'So I'd be grateful if you'd find another home for them.'

She brightened. 'Well, if you're going abroad, why don't I . . . ?'

'Don't even think of it.'

But he found himself smiling. 'Did you give your keys back to the caretaker?'

'No, why should I? You can take them back if you like. I must say, I didn't expect this. Is there any more coffee? As you can imagine, I've had a rather upsetting morning.'

He shook his head in admiration. 'You can leave your bags here on one condition, that you leave me your mobile number.' He realized that, as ever, she had asked him no questions about his plans. For this he was grateful: his plans were, as ever, unformed. But imperceptibly he could sense a growing desire to be elsewhere, whatever it cost, away from this greyness. He could no longer stand England, its cold, its coldness. In her fashion she had much to teach him. Rootlessness did not appear to disturb her, rather the opposite. She sat back in her chair, quite relaxed now that she had achieved her objective. And in truth the favours she asked were insignificant. It was just that she saw no reason why her wishes should not be granted. Others, no doubt, had found themselves in the same position, would face the same triumph of the will. Even now she was quite relaxed, bright-eyed, flicking her hair behind her ears, as he remembered her doing. He wondered if he could ever live with such a woman, and decided that it was impossible. Yet she was not easy to dismiss, and he was sure that many men had been attracted. She would be an intriguing partner, but not for long. He saw her days filled with endless soliloquies poured into the ears of defenceless friends. The difference between them was not simply one of temperament, but of age, or rather of generations. Only Sarah, he knew, would have shared his reactions in a similar circumstance. That was one of the ties that united them, that of age. And the coming age for both of them was one of austerity, not of indulgence.

'What will you do today?' he asked, anxious now to see her go.

'Look in on one or two people. My solicitor is taking me out to lunch. Why? Do you want to get rid of me?'

'I have things to do,' he said lamely. 'Papers to go through.' He wished it were true. 'It's been nice to see you.'

'I get the message,' she said. 'Well, I'll love you and leave you.'

'Your mobile number, Vicky.'

She reeled off the inconveniently long number, which he hastily wrote down. 'Perhaps you'll let me know when you're next in town. Your bags . . .'

'Don't worry. I know they're quite safe with you.'

They both laughed. There would be no need for further negotiations. No room either.

23

'Did you enjoy that?'

'Not much. A bit suburban, wasn't it?'

'That was the whole point. That was why I liked it. I am an inveterate suburbanite.'

'Oh, I know.'

They were lunching at the Tate, having paid their respects to an exhibition of paintings by the Camden Town Group.

'Even when I moved away from home I never really felt at home, if you know what I mean. It felt more natural to explore London as if I were a foreigner, different districts, you know? Pilgrimages to St Paul's, Westminster Abbey. I still thought of these as obligations, something Londoners ought to do. I was quite startled when tourists asked me directions, never felt I was in a position to advise them. Even now I never feel quite at home, but that's an old story. Homesickness. A chronic condition. Or maybe it increases with age. Do you want coffee?'

'Yes, please. Then I must go. I have to say, you don't look old. You've still got hair. You haven't put on weight. How do you manage that?'

'I don't eat much, I suppose. But then I don't know how much other people eat. I have no standards of comparison.'

'I eat all the wrong things, I know. Except when I'm in France.'

'Yes, how was your trip?'

'Oh, very brief. Just to check on the house. No need, really. I've got a local man who does odd jobs for me. He looks in from time to time.'

'When are you off again?'

'In a couple of weeks. I ought to sell the house, I suppose, but I can't bring myself to do it.'

'What happened to your husband?'

'He remarried, and then he died shortly after. Heart attack.'

'That must have been a blow.'

'It frightened me, certainly. But by that time I was rather ill myself. There are no good memories of that time. Just illness.'

'And now?'

'I suppose I've got into the habit of taking care of myself.'

'That's not good, Sarah. And so unlike you, that's what I can't get over. You never seemed to tire in the old days.'

'I know. Now I can't wait to get to bed. I sleep a lot.'

'I wish I could. I seem to have too much time on my hands. But I've come to dread the nights. Age again, I suppose. Sleep seems too close to death.'

'Must you?' She stirred restlessly. 'Shall we go?'

He sighed, picked up the bill. This excursion had not been a success. He had hoped to divert her, but in fact she was visibly tired. He himself had not been as enthusiastic as he had hoped, had been distracted, unable or unwilling to give the pictures his full attention. The truth was that they were both conscious of their own histories, unable to escape from their memories. And not simply of their memories of each other, but of themselves. This was a particularly cruel realization, and one which they seemed to share. Was this to be the pattern of the future, an unnerving self-consciousness? Her presence now, so longed for in years gone by, was unredeemed by any desire for future company. He sensed that she was anxious to get away from him, simply because he communicated a sense of the past being irrecoverable. He himself felt this, and it struck him as a tragedy. He wished that he could have seen the pictures on his own, despite his diminished response. Instead he had felt her weight on his arm, had felt obliged to support her, and increasingly irritated by her stick. She was right: they were better off on their own now. And yet what sadness to relinquish their past in this fashion. Was love merely an intrinsic part of youthful energy? It seemed that she had made her peace with this conclusion more willingly than he had. Maybe women were more realistic than men, maybe that was why they lived longer. But what hell they must endure in their selfishly guarded but lamentable old age.

He steered her carefully through the crowds and into the open air, where they both paused to catch their breath.

'Shall we walk a bit? You don't have any appointments this afternoon, do you?'

'Of course I don't. Thank you for lunch, by the way.'

'Be careful on these steps.'

'Oh, Paul. You're such an old woman. I'm not entirely senile.'

Offended, he knew for the hundredth time that she was irritated by what was intended as loving concern, though truth to tell he felt little of that at the prospect of irritating her yet again, felt a certain weariness on his own behalf. Left alone he would have walked home, dissipating his own feelings of regret. He steered her carefully round the young people sitting on the steps, reached the pavement with a sense of deliverance. They were silent, anticipating the solitude that they both craved. They greeted the arrival of a taxi with relief.

'I'll take you home,' he said.

'There's no need. If you want to walk . . .'

'No, no. I'll walk later. I've plenty of time.'

They both smiled, but said nothing further. He noticed, with a slight return of pleasure, pigeons going about their business in the chilly streets. Nature, it seemed, was about to replace art. It might help if there were any reduction in the greyness of the weather, but this spring was bleak, with frequent rain showers. Again this seemed symbolic. He sighed; this was how he had felt in the school holidays, all those years ago. Beside him Sarah was suddenly a stranger, apparently attentive to the view beyond the window, no more eager to talk than he was. The sight of those young people – students, he supposed – sitting on the steps, had irritated him even further. To be young again was a wish that could never be granted. He was almost glad that he knew no young people. Children were a different matter, but he knew no children either. He began to understand the disappointments that had so changed Sarah, the sense of failure at not having brought about this fundamental procedure. Not that she would have made an ideal mother, but her tonic indifference would have been something of a gift to any son she might have had, made him into the sort of man she admired, tough, restless, self-reliant. Now, as then, she had no use for any other kind of man. His very loyalty told against him. Fidelity had never been an attribute she admired. Some of the worst misunderstandings of their lives had been occasioned by this very divergence. Despite any virtue he might have had as her admirer he could never overcome this fundamental failure.

'Careful,' he warned, as she stepped heavily out of the taxi. 'That stick is a hindrance, if you ask me. Careful,' he repeated, as she stumbled.

'My ankle. Oh, God, my ankle.'

'Lean on me. Just let me pay the taxi.'

'It's sprained. I know it's sprained.'

'Let's get inside. Or would you rather go to the hospital?'

'Oh, never again. I'll die here.'

'Don't be ridiculous, Sarah. You've twisted your ankle. There's no need to panic.'

Bearing her full weight he guided her into the house and settled her in a chair, noting for the first time how gloomy the room was: red walls, heavy curtains, a vague gesture in the direction of the more prestigious houses she had known in her youth. He knelt down in front of her, in a parody of allegiance, like a page before his knight, gently moved the ankle from side to side.

'It's not broken,' he said firmly, remembering incidents from the school playground. 'I doubt if it's even sprained. If it were you couldn't move it. It may need some sort of bandage. Or something cold. Can you take off your stockings?'

Unwillingly he watched her struggling with her clothes, marvelling at the ungainliness so very different from her manner of undressing – swift, unhesitating – in earlier years. The sight of her bare legs, the now swollen ankle, moved him not to pity but to a certain reluctance. He had not been meant to witness this. Yet she seemed willing to abandon her former pride, rather more than he would have expected her to do. Living alone had not made her stoical: rather the opposite. What she was experiencing was not pain, but fear. Her expression was one of acute anxiety, as if this small injury marked the end of her life as a viable individual. This must have been the effect of her long period of illness. No wonder she was changed.

'How's it feeling now?'

'A little better. I didn't want you to see me like this.'

'You know I've seen you many times before . . .'

'Not like this.'

'No, not like this, perhaps. But anyone can have an accident. No one is safe. Do you want me to stay?'

'No, not really. I'll just rest for a bit.'

'Can I call a neighbour?'

'Maria will be here shortly. My cleaner. She comes every

day. Although I don't want to rely on her.' She smiled faintly. 'It's come to this.'

'You've got me,' he said soberly. Yet he felt, along with his old devotion, an unreadiness. Why could he not have stayed quietly at home instead of devising this pointless excursion? What had the Tate to do with this scene of ugly domesticity? They would do better to avoid such activities in future, or indeed all activities which involved such a high degree of uncertainty. In this respect she had been the wiser of the two, dismissing his suggestions, ignoring his hearty reproaches. But perhaps he himself tended to be too cautious, as if cautiousness led to weakness. Looking at Sarah now he saw how easily the scales might be tipped, how little separated them from each other. It was in his interest now to get away from this ungainly spectacle, even to get away from memories which he had thought indelible. His own survival now depended on a wariness which he had not known before, certainly not in relation to this last attachment. His hand remained on her ankle, in a gesture of appeasement. Instinct told him to breathe in a less compromised air, to get out, to walk as he was accustomed to walking, as if nothing could ever stop him. To stay any longer in this red room was to accept confinement, not merely to sympathize, but worse, to empathize, to mimic this fallen condition. Never had he so longed to be away, to preserve his autonomy in surroundings which held no memory. He removed his hand, stood up.

'You're looking better,' he said, as much for his own sake as for hers. But it was true: colour was back in her cheeks. Her look of exhaustion gave her an unusual gravity. These portents affected him as much as they had affected her. He wondered how long he could endure if she were to die. More pointedly he wondered how soon he could leave.

The sound of a key in the door brought the hiatus to an

end. A small dark woman bustled into the room, and almost immediately the air was filled with lamentations. This must be Maria, the lamentations her prompt reaction to the sight of her employer almost supine in her chair. The two women embraced, which rather shocked Sturgis: the Sarah he knew would not have countenanced such a contact. He stood up awkwardly, his presence now redundant. Sarah, he was interested to see, was rapidly recovering some of her old dominance. Indeed he was almost forgotten, or at least marginalized. The two women were intent only on each other, Sarah pretending to ridicule Maria's easy tears, but secretly accepting them as her due.

'Perhaps you could make a cup of tea,' he suggested.

They both looked at him in surprise, as if they had forgotten he was there.

'Yes, I make tea.'

'Anything you need, Sarah, let me know. Shopping, of course I can do all that. I'll ring you later, call round in the morning. I'll leave you with Maria.'

'I call doctor.'

'I'm sure there's no need,' he began, but then decided to leave them to it.

As ever he was glad to reach the blessed anonymity of the street. This was his climate, the everyday, the spectacle of others absorbed in thoughts different from his own. What he had witnessed was incapacity, the same incapacity his mother had demonstrated in her declining years. He concentrated on the reality of his present surroundings, the sight of a bus, the promise of the evening paper. It was drizzling now, but he walked on. She would be fine, he reassured himself. And if she were not he would find others to help. There was no onus on him to assume exclusive responsibility. He was shocked to discover that it was his own survival that now had priority.

Never before had he suspected himself of such meanness of spirit. Perhaps this was one of the no doubt unwelcome surprises that awaited him. A telephone call would be adequate, he decided. Then, in the morning, he would take a view.

There was a message on his answering machine. 'Hi, Vicky here. Just to say don't worry if you don't see me for a bit. I've been invited to stay with friends in L.A. Hope to pick up some useful contacts. See you! Ciao!'

24

There followed an interval of near-domestic concord. Every morning he bought supplies at the Italian shop, as he had done before, but more expansively. 'What have you brought?' was her usual greeting, though she quickly lost interest. After a few days this changed to, 'That's too much for me. You'd better stay and share it with me.' In the kitchen he divided the food – ham, cheese, salads – into two, and took the plates back into the red room, where she sat immobile, her ankle swathed in a white bandage, her foot on a low stool. If there was a dining-room he had yet to see it. Part of him deplored this laissez-faire attitude; privately he thought she should be making more of an effort. Don't let me be like that, he silently addressed some problematic or disputatious deity. Yet her tone was as uncompromising as ever. This, if anything, was a relief. He washed up, parcelled up the rubbish, and awaited further orders.

'You might as well go,' she would say, but there were the old unmistakable signs that she expected him to protest. After a time she became more discursive, referred to some business she had to see to.

'Business?'

'The usual things. Daddy put me on the board of one or two of his companies before he died. I go to the meetings, the dinners, that sort of thing. Not that I can do that now. It doesn't look as if I'll be able to go to France, either.'

'What did the doctor say?'

'Just to rest it. Keep the foot up. I've never been so bored in my life.'

'Any visitors?'

'Only you.' There was no mistaking that tone. 'Not that I'm not grateful.'

He supposed that she was, though she gave little sign of that. Yet he could not bring himself to leave her unattended. He would stay until Maria arrived, when she would become her old self, relaxing with some satisfaction into the reliable routine of mistress and servant. As he closed the door behind him he would hear her voice gaining authority, the hallmark of her circle in the old days. Once, calling for her at her office in her father's headquarters, he had been impressed by the ringing tones of various secretaries, most of them her old schoolfriends. She, and no doubt they, were working there as temporary assistants. They seemed to do a reasonable job of work, though this was interrupted from time to time by the holidays they took, mostly with one another. This was apparently part of the routine, to which their employers gracefully submitted. Once, four of them had hired a camper van and set off to tour Greece. No one appeared to take exception to this. It was in keeping with the flippant attitude they took towards their bosses, to which their bosses seemed to subscribe. This was, after all, a family affair, and the pattern of behaviour had no doubt lingered from boarding school. Heads were no doubt shaken at management level, but with an indulgent smile. No word of criticism was ever heard. And the work got done quite efficiently, or so he supposed. They were not without resource, these girls, as relaxed about obeying the rules as they were about breaking them.

That had been the climate of their earliest encounters. Even now she seemed inseparable from that company, or perhaps simply from that sort of company, those confident voices. They all got married at about the same time, to the same sort of man. That was when he felt at his most ill-equipped, genetically unable to match that confidence. His own early associations had been modest, local, tenacious. He had been accepted, to his surprise, with some provisos. The only real surprise was that he had stayed. And he was somehow still present, carefully stacking plates in her kitchen, still a reluctant admirer of all that he secretly disliked, still instinctively objecting to all that she stood for, still loyal to his original adoration, but at the same time restless, with the same restlessness that had originally affected him on being introduced to her friends, whose allusions escaped him and had probably been instilled at birth.

'Do you ever see those girls you used to know?' he asked, picking up the plastic bags in which he had brought the shopping.

'Jane? Clare? Oh, occasionally, though they're all scattered now. Nobody lives in town now. Richard and I used this place as a bolthole. We were mainly in France. We had them to stay once or twice, but they had children, and we more or less lost touch.'

He suspected that she had distanced herself from those friends when they successfully gave birth to children. With this he could sympathize.

Maria's key in the door put an end to the morning's attendance. 'I'll see you tomorrow,' he said.

'No, not tomorrow. I'm being taken out to lunch. One of Richard's friends from the old days.'

'How will you manage?'

'We shall see. He'll drive, of course. In fact, don't think you have to come every day. I'm sure there's plenty of food.'

'There's plenty of food, yes. It's in the fridge.'

'Then don't come for a few days. Why don't you look in at the weekend?'

'Will you be all right on your own?'

'I'm used to it. Maria will stay if I need her.'

'Well, then, I'll see you at the weekend. You can always ring me if you . . .'

'Yes, yes. Do go, Paul. You're making me nervous, standing over me like that.'

He kissed her cheek, reassured to see her face lifted expectantly, then left, not without a sense of relief. The street, for once, failed to revive him, seemed, on the contrary, to hold him prisoner in a routine which he now saw as unavoidable. He glanced with distaste at the unchanging grey skies, and put his malaise down to the absence of the sun. He felt as grimly conditioned by these skies as any conscript, and, scanning the faces of passers-by, captured something of the same disappointment, from which only a different climate could deliver them.

Reaching home at the dead hour between three and four did little to sweeten his mood. The interruption to his days had resolved nothing. He supposed that Sarah was glad of the attention, was even grateful for it, but was too proud to acknowledge it, whereas her company had severed his links with his habitual solitude. He was at a loss, in more ways than one. He had to acknowledge the fact that their attachment, their friendship, was little more than a relic of the past. She had clearly seen this much earlier, how much earlier he did not care to think. He supposed that he fulfilled some sort of function in her life, but was shamed by his own persistence, which was all too obviously an irritant. She could always telephone if she needed him. That, after all, had always been the arrangement.

Yet a few days later, on what he had already decided would be his last visit, he found her agitated. The bandage had gone, but she was still immobile. He felt the beginnings of a yawn as he sat down opposite her, and prepared, yet again, to sympathize.

'How have you been?' he enquired.

'I'm all right in the daytime. But the nights are bad. And

I have bad dreams. Although they're not so much dreams as memories.'

'My dreams are like that. I used to find them quite interesting. Now I'm not so sure.'

'For instance, last night I woke in a panic. And it wasn't a dream that woke me. It was a memory. I remembered I had forgotten to lock the garden door when I left. And I can't go there to see to it.'

'You said there was an odd-job man.'

'Yes, but I don't like him in the house when I'm not there. I don't know how far I can trust him.'

'Surely, in an emergency . . . But you're probably imagining the whole thing.'

'No, I'm not. I distinctly remember being in a hurry – I forget why – and anxious to get away. I was wondering . . .' she looked away, 'if you could pop down there for me? I know it's a lot to ask. There'd be nothing to do when you got there, just to double-lock the garden door, although you could stay if you wanted to. No, on second thoughts, wait till I'm back there. I always intended to invite you.'

'You did mention it. But this hardly seems sensible. Anyway, how could I get in?'

'I'd give you a set of keys, of course. You could hang on to them until I see you again. Or you could post them back. That was the arrangement when we lent the house to friends. Richard kept a stack of registered envelopes which he handed out. He was very security conscious. And you always liked to go to France, didn't you?'

'I haven't been for some time.'

'Well, now's your chance. Do say you will, Paul. It would relieve my mind. Here.' She opened the drawer of a small table and took out a set of keys. 'Do go, Paul. I wouldn't trust anyone else. And I obviously can't go myself. It's quite easy to find. The house, I mean. You fly to Nice and take a bus to Saint-Paul. Or a taxi, of course. Though if you take a taxi ask him to wait: they're not too easy to find. I imagine you won't want to linger. Just make sure you lock all the doors when you leave.'

He hesitated. He could raise no objection to her plan, apart from the fact that it was her plan and not his. But he was not in principle averse to the idea. He would have little to do once his inspection was completed. And he would be free to stay, if not in Saint-Paul then in Nice, which he knew well. He looked at the card she had given him, along with the keys: 121 *bis* rue Grande. But already he was thinking of Nice. With a sudden ache he remembered taking his coffee in the Place Masséna, the dazzling light, the sense of purpose. In that wide space, under those skies, one could not help but feel free, domestic associations left far behind. And then one could stay in an hotel, rediscover the delights of sheer rootlessness. Somewhere, he thought, was the ideal hotel, one that he would recognize from his fantasies. What he would do when he found it was unclear, but as a fantasy it was no less plausible than the marriage he had concocted for himself, on no other basis than his desire for change. He felt ashamed of this made-up life, contrasted it with the realities of the present, with Sarah's impatient face, and with the envelope in his hand.

'So what do you say? Or rather, how soon can you go? I am rather anxious, Paul. And I don't suppose you're busy.'

'Why don't you suppose that? Though in fact you're right. I rather like to plan my visits, but there's no reason why I shouldn't go tomorrow if necessary.'

'It would relieve my mind.'

'Very well. I'll give you a call. Either from France, or more probably when I'm back.'

'And post the keys once you've locked up.'

'Very well. I'll leave you now. You'll take care, I hope.'

'Yes, yes. Why do you make such a fuss over everything?'

'You know, Sarah, we might be an old married couple.'

'You mean, I sound like a nagging wife.'

'You do, rather. Come to think of it you always did.'

They both laughed. 'That's better,' she said. 'But do go soon. And ring me.'

There never was, surely, such a late spring. He walked through streets indistinguishable from those he had walked through all winter. A sharp wind threatened the early blossom: he walked through a scurry of pink petals, some already stuck to the damp pavement. He noted how cleverly they had side-stepped the important issues: how they would cope when they were really old, really infirm, when her house stood empty in perpetuity and he could no longer travel at her or indeed his behest. Perhaps this was the true legacy of her illness, the fear that she might be left unaccompanied in a hostile world. He would play his part as long as he could, would try to allay fears which he shared. The past now seemed too distant to be relevant. Time was accelerating, and in the light of the present the past seemed overlaid by a sense of failure. He did not doubt that she was aware of this. She had always been intensely practical: that ringing laugh, those commanding tones were not mere mannerisms but the out-come of legitimate expectations. Now there were no more expectations. Even women who were accustomed to success would know that at some point the line had been drawn. And he was hardly the man to disabuse her. For all his reassurances he was in no position to redress the balance.

And for himself the future held little more than the grim routines that had always sustained him, together with the hope that they would sustain him to the end. Then it would be time to rely on the kindness of strangers, and the hope that this would prove more than a fond illusion. For this reason if for no other he welcomed the prospect of a diversion, tiresome though it might turn out to be. He would do the minimum, check the doors, and leave, seek his reward in the sun. For surely he could rely on the sun? In such longed-for benefits he would place his trust, having little to invest elsewhere.

He reached home just as the clouds disgorged a shower. He discarded his unread newspaper. He checked his currency, booked a return flight to Nice. Despite the odd flare of nostalgia, he foresaw difficulties in such a precipitate departure. As a tourist he might have welcomed the excursion, but he was tired, his legacy of bad nights suddenly an unconscionable weight. He packed a small bag, skirting his way round Mrs Gardner's bags, which now had the appearance of a permanent fixture. Out of curiosity he undid them, something he had not done before. The larger of the two held a towelling bathrobe and a pair of high-heeled boots, the smaller a radio with a dead battery and two pairs of shoes. What she did with her clothes he had no idea, maybe left them at her husband's house as a gage of her return. He imagined her belongings stashed away safely in other people's houses, much as she might have put them into storage. It was as good a way as any of keeping them under her control, and, as he had had time to find out, she was indifferent to any inconvenience this might cause. She had at least left him her mobile number, but he did not particularly want her to know that his flat would be empty. Nevertheless he made the call. There was no reply. But yet again he could not prevent himself from smiling. That was the way to leave, with nothing of value left behind. It was a lesson that he might do well to learn.

25

The house was in a small cul-de-sac off the rue Grande. Contrary to what he expected it was an ugly yellow villa with blue railings and a large integral garage. One half of the roof was flat, the other a rakish diagonal. He recognized its origins in the brutalist architecture of the 1930s, no doubt a prime example of Art Deco, and therefore *classé*, protected from being in any way altered or modified.

The interior was no more welcoming. Stiff blinds, which he did not disturb, obscured what light there was. A long passage led from the front to the rear of the house, where a glass door admitted a little more light. This door, the one in question, he supposed, was securely locked. He tested it with the keys he had been given, opened and shut it, and locked it again. After that he decided that his mission was completed.

Repelled by the house's angularity he felt no desire to linger, was in fact anxious to find the taxi which was parked some way away. It was already evening; he was aware of crowds sitting on terraces. He supposed he might have stayed, found a hotel room nearby, taken his time about returning. Instead he told the driver to take him back to Nice, where he would be obliged to spend the night. Yet even Nice was less to his taste than he remembered it, noisier, more crowded, the hotels full. He was forced to spend more money than he had bargained for, in one of the larger hotels, where he felt lamentably out of place. He spent the rest of the evening in his room, willing the time to pass until he could leave. Home seemed incredibly distant, unreachable. There was nothing here to detain him. Clearly the expected transformation had not materialized. He slept badly, distracted by the murmur of conversation from an adjoiining room, the squeal of a trolley delivering someone's room service. He was up at first light, roused a night porter to pay his bill, and left with an audible sigh of relief. This was not it, not it at all. The illusion had, once again, proved superior to the reality.

A flight to London had just left. By now he was febrile, took the next flight to Paris, was determined to travel the rest of the way by train. This had been a wasted journey, and a disappointing one, failing to deliver the expected rush of feeling, or even the dull satisfaction of a task successfully carried out. The house had been inimical, totally different from the picturesque *cottage orné* he had led himself to expect. Art Deco had always struck him as unfriendly, an artificial style, suitable for Bright Young Things, a setting only for cocktail parties. He supposed that the house was valuable, but doubted that it could ever inspire affection. Yet Sarah seemed to cherish it, having wrested it away from her mother-in-law in a skirmish which now seemed prehistoric. There was an untold story here of wrangled-over succession which made it seem even less attractive. He revised his long-held belief that some families were happier or more harmonious than others. It seemed that only in the blessed state of infancy was one unquestioningly accepting. After that it was a matter of adjustment, or simply of transferring one's expectations, trying to find another home for them, but always conscious of being somehow disinherited.

Paris was reassuring, more accommodating than Nice, and strangely quieter. Here the associations were more pleasant. He had first come here as a school leaver, on his first adult holiday. He had been allowed this brief licence by his parents on condition that he was accompanied by his friend Tom

Williamson, and that he did not drink anything. In fact it was Tom who got drunk, and this incidentally caused him to reflect that he would rather have been not necessarily with someone else, for he was fond of Tom, but perhaps with a girl, who would have been gentler company. This conviction had carried on into true adulthood. He was happier with women than with men, looking for that combination of respect and pleasure that he instinctively sought. And sometimes found, though too rarely to assume a longing it was now time to forgo.

Almost amused, he made his way to the rue Madame, where he and Tom had been supposed to share a room in the apartment of an elderly widow. This had been arranged by his father through a contact at the bank. They had decided immediately that this was unsuitable and had decamped to a nearby hotel, thus occasioning massive disfavour at home. It was a rite of passage that had served them both well, though they lost sight of each other when Tom went on to study medicine and he became a wage earner. But the holiday remained significant, a promise of what was to come. And Paris remained welcoming, though he was disappointed to note that their original hotel had been refurbished. This, if anything, signified the end of youthful naïveté, though it was strange how awkwardly this persisted. One continued to hope, however misplaced that hope might be. He supposed he might now go home, was conscious of his bag, and the keys in his pocket, but not quite ready to confront his all too familiar flat. Instead he crossed the street to a café for coffee, then went back and booked a room. 'Pour combien de temps?' asked the woman at the desk. 'Une nuit seulement,' he replied.

He was tired now, his legs significantly weaker. The idea of a long walk, always his routine when he was in Paris, repelled him. In the mirror of his room he noted his drawn face, the features sombre, devoid of his habitual mild smile. And there were other signs that he might not have been aware of, his parched-looking skin, his thinning hair. The evidence was all too clear: he could undertake no more excursions. He lay down on the bed, let himself drift off into sleep, not without a sense of nightmare. But this was standard now, and the pull of sleep was too strong to be resisted. He knew he had urgent business to see to, should telephone Sarah and book a ticket to London. He even wondered whether he had really locked those doors, felt for the keys on the bedside table, assured himself that they were where he had left them. Sleep overtook him once more, and he slept with his arm slipping to the floor, no longer sure of where he was, or where he would be when he awoke.

Two hours later he emerged from a dreamless trance, feeling oddly free of his usual anxiety. He deduced that his troubles were caused by simple fatigue, and without hesitation removed his clothes and got into the bed. Again he slept, almost at once, surfacing from time to time, but untroubled by the alien sounds of the hotel going about its business. This was a welcome departure from his silent nights at home, in which the absence of sound was more disturbing than any interference. He felt unusually comforted by the sounds of doors opening and closing, by a woman's laughter, a man's reassuring rumble. Though far removed from his usual hermetic surroundings, he drifted gratefully into a different kind of relaxation, one in which he could be sure that if necessary others would supply his needs. In one particularly lucid interval he recognized that this was what he had always envisaged, the hotel merely a symbol of a temporary and therefore realistic existence. The idea, then, had not been planted in his consciousness without reason. He had time to marvel at this process, which underlay his usual fantasizing, being less

intended, more convincing, and even devoid of his own volition. Having overcome any objections or prevarications his
conscious mind might have devised for him, he slept again, to
be awakened by the bright light of a fine morning. He reckoned
he had slept for nearly nine hours.

He bathed, dressed, asked for a *café complet*, which was
delivered promptly by a sour-faced maid. With her lack of
salutation the real world renewed its demands. Traffic started
up in the street, the working day already under way. He put
through a call to London, was surprised to be answered by an
angry voice. He looked at his watch: seven-thirty, clearly too
early for civilized discussion. Yet the light called to him, and
in the light the room looked shabbier than it had done the
previous day. He was free to leave, but at the same time
unwilling to go home. The voice in his ear suggested that he
was at fault, that Sarah, being woken from sleep, was even
less amenable than he remembered. He cleared his throat,
downed the rest of his coffee.

'Sarah? It's Paul.'

'Do you know what time it is?'

'I do now. I'm sorry if I woke you. It's a fine day here.'

'Where are you?'

'In Paris. I'm not sure when I'll be back. But all's well.'

'Did you lock up?'

'Of course I locked up. That's what I was there for. But in
fact the door was safely locked anyway. I had nothing to do
there, so I came back to Paris.'

'I see. Well, thank you. That's one worry off my mind.'

'I don't intend to make a habit of this, Sarah. You'll have to
make other arrangements if you can't manage on your own.
With the caretaker, or whatever he is. There was no sign of him,
incidentally. No sign of anyone, come to that. I was quite glad
to get away. Why on earth are you so attached to the place?'

'Well, it belonged to Richard, or rather to his family, as I told you. His mother handed it over when we married.'

'Why don't you sell it? I thought it hideous, if you really want to know. And I don't doubt you'd get a good price for it.'

'I can't go into that now, though the idea had occurred to me. Perhaps we could discuss it. Or you could advise me.'

'I just have advised you.'

'All right, all right. You wouldn't like to buy it yourself?'

'Why should I do that?'

'Well, you always used to say you wouldn't mind retiring to France.'

'That was a long time ago.'

'Well, why not?'

'No reason. Sarah, I'll give you a ring when I get back to London. Tomorrow or the next day. I'm rather anxious to go out at the moment.' A pause. 'You're all right?'

'More or less.'

'The ankle?'

'A bit better. It was sprained, you know.'

'Yes, yes.' He did not want to dwell on infirmities, not in the clear grey light, the light he always considered native to Paris, at the window. 'I'll see you soon. Take care of yourself.'

He broke off with a sensation of deliverance, though the deliverance was short-lived. Her voice brought back to him all those unwilling associations usually subsumed under the heading 'home'. Had he still had a desk to go to he would have scrutinized the matter, put it on paper, and filed it away. This was no longer possible. But by the same token there was no one to call him to account. He was to all intents and purposes a free man, but a man for whom freedom was not entirely comfortable.

Refreshed by this exchange of views, and by the fact that

he had managed to state his position in the teeth of her suggestions, he went down to the desk, and told the concierge, *'Je reste encore une nuit.'* This surprised him no less than his firmness on the telephone, as did his suspicion that Sarah, having conceived the idea on the spur of the moment, might raise the matter of his buying the house when she next saw him. Even if he could afford to pay for the house the idea was ludicrous. The house was not merely a relic but isolated. And it was her idea, rather than his. He shook his head, not without a smile. This was how she had always been.

He walked down to the river, under a brightening sky, crossed the Cour du Louvre to Palais Royal, and sat down at an outdoor café. It was still early, and his walk had stimulated his appetite. Freed from his normal routine he was able to invent himself, a gift he thought he had lost. He nodded to a man at the next table who nodded back. Affability, not much practised in England, was still current in France. He did not mistake this holiday mood for any more decisive change, but was disposed to make the most of it for the space of a day, or even two days. He decided to give the Louvre a miss, which he thought he was now entitled to do. No one seemed to take him to account for this improvised existence. London was far away, indistinct. The distance he had recently covered had, after all, fulfilled some sort of function, though he was too canny to misinterpret this. He crossed the bridge, putting the Louvre definitively behind him, and on impulse caught a bus, not knowing or caring where it took him. Within minutes, it seemed, it reached what appeared to be a terminus, in a wide street apparently within reach of a large green space: the Bois, he assumed. He could go to the Musée Marmottan, but decided against it, much as he had turned his back on the Louvre. Works of art belonged in a different category to his present condition. His inclination was to stay in the pleasant streets until sheer tiredness forced him to return to the hotel in the rue Madame, which was in no sense the hotel of his fantasies. Maybe no hotel could live up to that image. But even less than the ideal hotel did his flat represent an agreeable alternative. That life of making do, of making the best of a comfortable but uncomforting existence, could no longer be sustained. He supposed that he would go back to it eventually, but seen from here it registered as a last resort, rather like a hospital, or rather in the same category as a hospital, a place to die. And with a returning chill he confronted the always unacceptable truth, that there would be no one there at the end.

He made his way down a populous street, where a market appeared to be taking place. This was, or seemed to be, a wealthy district: of the legendary turbulence of the outer suburbs there was no sign or suspicion. The spectacle was absorbing. He envied those who lived within reach of such plenty, such easy exchange. His present displacement was oddly satisfying, so that what was in reality lack of purpose was no longer a burden. He put this down to the benign weather, the absence of cloud, but in fact it had more to do with this street, the feeling of being off-centre, away from the nominal heart of Paris. He wondered if he might stay here rather than in the rue Madame. It would be a matter of half an hour, merely, to retrieve his bag. He looked around for an hotel, and saw one. It seemed, from the outside, pleasant enough. But this was not it, not it at all. Another solution must be found. Only if that solution escaped him would he admit defeat.

He was tiring once again. He left this entirely congenial place and wandered without direction, almost reconciled to the knowledge of his impermanence. He found himself in a small quiet street, the rue Berton, he noted. On a discreet grey façade he saw a small plaque: Pension Franklin. At that moment the door opened and a pleasant middle-aged woman emerged, wished him '*Bonjour*', and hurried away. He pushed open the door into a silent lobby, looked around, waited for someone to appear. This, he thought, might be acceptable. For a week, for a month, maybe for longer.

'*Vous désirez une chambre?*' enquired a voice. He came out of his reverie to find himself addressed by a man of his own age, formally dressed, and carrying a newspaper, a man not unlike himself on a good day. This must be the manager, or perhaps the owner, though there was no hint of any commerce involved.

'*Une chambre? Oui, peut-être. Mais je dois partir ce soir. Je vous téléphonerai de Londres.*'

'*Comme vous voulez.*'

He hesitated. '*La nuit porte conseil*,' said the man, handing him a card. And indeed the previous night, that night without dreams, had delivered something of a verdict. In the absence of any other he accepted this as a sign.

26

Home, as Philip Larkin memorably observed, is so sad. It stays as it was left. He looked round his flat, at the books he would never read again, mute testimonies to former enthusiasms. A tap dripped in the kitchen. He would have to do something about that, which meant his usual polite pleas to the caretaker, who was always doing something somewhere else, and to whom he would have to deploy his usual interested enquiries, masking his request behind a show of interest in the man's activities. There were books, more books to be taken back to the London Library, laundry to be dealt with, supplies of a sort to be bought, the newspapers, which he had forgotten to cancel, to be disposed of. And Sarah's keys to be returned: that was his most pressing obligation, the one he was most eager to discharge. The image of that yellow house, mutely inhospitable, obstinately silent, repelled him even more than it had done when he had locked the door behind him. It spoke of activities which he had no desire to investigate, had a history which excluded him entirely. He felt retrospectively annoyed that he had allowed himself to be pressed into service. More so than at any other time, perhaps, he deplored his own disposition, his loyalties, even his desire for friendship. But if he were to move, to act on his wager, that desire might be renewed.

He found Sarah in the position in which he had left her, apparently immobile in her ugly red room. He was aware of a change in her appearance, put it down to the fact that her hair was less cared for than usual, that the grey was now dominant. She saw him looking at her, gave a weary smile, put her hand to her head.

'I couldn't quite face the hairdresser,' she said. 'Is it that obvious?'

'I could take you, if you want to make an appointment.'

'All those women chattering. I don't think so.'

'At least let me take you out for coffee. You should get some air.'

She glanced out of the window. 'Not very tempting, is it? It looks like rain.'

It was indeed grey, warm but humid. The weather forecaster, to whom he had listened before leaving the flat, was indomitably cheerful, though promising heavy showers. Soldier on, seemed to be the message.

'You didn't feel like staying, then?'

'No, though I may go back. Oh, let me give you the keys.'

'Back?'

'Back to Paris. I need a break, Sarah. And there's nothing to keep me here. Unless you . . .'

'I thought of going away myself. We travelled so much in the past. In the old days, I nearly said.'

'I'm afraid the old days are really over now.'

'There's only my sister-in-law left. Richard's sister, Mary. Very limited woman. We kept in touch, more or less. So I gave her a ring. I'm going to stay with her for a bit.'

'Where?'

'Near Chichester. Not that I'm looking forward to it. But I need more help, Paul. More care. And she was always very sociable. Dinner parties, and so on. I shan't be alone. That's what I can no longer stand.'

'How long will you stay there?'

'No idea. Until we get tired of each other, I suppose. I was never one for much female company. But when you get older you miss it, if only for purposes of comparison. I dare say it's different for a man.'

'Why should it be? Life gets lonelier; that's the truth of the matter. In fact that adds to the disappointment. I suppose most lives end in disappointment.'

'Must you?'

'That's why I thought I'd go back to Paris for a bit. A change of scene. I don't want to spend the rest of my life in my flat. In fact I've taken against it.'

'About time too.'

'I know you never liked it. It meant so much to me when I first bought it, promised all sorts of freedoms. But in fact freedom is rather like silence: one can have too much of it. Do come out, Sarah. I find this room rather oppressive.'

'The car is coming for me at half-past ten.'

'Whose car?'

'The car I ordered, of course.'

'You mean you're going today? This morning?'

'No reason to stay here. Thank you for the keys, though you could have posted them.'

'When will I see you again?'

'I'm not sure. I'll ring you.'

'But I may not be here.'

They looked at each other in astonishment. The same idea occurred to both of them simultaneously. To be out of touch was a grave risk. Behind this desire for change lay the need to make plans, to make arrangements. Sarah, more practical than himself, had had less hesitation that he had shown, with his airy notion of exile. He had hoped to discuss this with Sarah, had hoped for some kind of comment, perhaps some measure of regret. In fact this had been forestalled by news of her own departure. This he had not bargained for.

'We were getting used to each other again.'

'Yes. That frightened me. I didn't want that.'

'Very flattering.'

'Oh, don't take offence. It's just that the idea of doing it all over again, all the same arguments, the same reasons . . . I can't go back to the beginning, Paul. I can't be young again. I can't give in to weakness, make a habit of you, as I once did.' They were both silent. 'Not that you'd want me now.'

'I still want you in my life.'

'There's no need to look like that. I'll be back. I have no doubt Mary will throw me out when she feels like it. We were never all that close. But she was amusing. Not your type. And you'll be back.'

'Back?'

'From Paris. Though what you think you'll be doing there I can't imagine.'

'I just had this vision of another way of life. Making it new. Foolish, I dare say. But as you've remarked, there's nothing to keep me here.'

'No, that's what I said about me.'

They smiled again.

'Promise me you'll come back.'

'Oh, I dare say I'll come home in the end. As you will.'

'You're sure you won't come out? Now, I mean. This room is almost as bad as my flat.'

'It is, isn't it. No, as I said, the car is coming at ten-thirty.'

'You got as far as ordering the car? Without waiting to tell me?'

'I left a message on your machine. Didn't you check it? I'll let you know when I'm back. Now, I'm afraid I'm going to let you go, Paul. I'll see you when I see you. Don't linger. You never did know when to leave.'

He walked thoughtfully, impressed by the simultaneity of their thinking. Surely that signified some connection, a resolve, a fear that they were not ready to confide to each other. They had assured one another that they would be back, but there was no guarantee of that. If Fate or nature were to be kind they would come together again. But Fate is rarely kind, and nature never. '*La nuit porte conseil*,' the man had said. But no advice had been forthcoming. Sarah, he knew, would make herself unaccommodating; there would soon be friction in that house in Chichester, but maybe that very friction would restore her self-belief, would prove to her that her character was intact. As for himself he had no such resource. His vision of his life in Paris had now dwindled almost to invisibility. And yet he knew that he could not stay here, in this grey city, surrounded by dire pronouncements, and those streets he once so conscientiously explored. Many of his former colleagues, he knew, had bought houses in France, in Spain, looking forward to a life in the sun, far from everything that was too familiar, too stale. The same desire for a better life, or at least for a different life, probably visited everyone once satisfied with what had been worked for, the same longing for some sort of reward, the same defiance, the same claim to more life. That was one of the dubious endowments of ageing, a conviction that one's desires had not been met, that there was in fact no reward, and that the way ahead was simply one of endurance. One or two of them had sold up and come home, not quite willing to give their reasons. As for the rest they had removed themselves from the picture and were thus doubly lost to view.

In the flat he collected the books from his bedside table, inevitably stubbing his toe on Mrs Gardner's luggage, now, he assumed, a permanent fixture. Eventually he would get rid of it, put it into storage somewhere, or leave it where it was. He had no further feeling for his flat, would have been profoundly grateful to be supplied with an alternative. He even had a brief moment of nostalgia for that old house, his first home, no happier in truth than the flat in which he had spent so many years, but now in hindsight bigger, weightier, more complex geographically than his present reduced space, the views from the windows more satisfying. But he knew that if he were to go back he would find a very ordinary setting, a largish house, certainly, but one in which he could no longer see himself. Only the power of dreams would deliver more to him than had already existed so long ago that he might still have been the age he was then, with a child's perception of size, miraculously recaptured under the influence of the night. It was daylight that restored life to its true proportions, and the life he rediscovered on waking had proved deceptive.

He set out for the London Library thinking of Sarah. 'I need more help,' she had said. 'I need more care.' He groaned at the implication of these remarks, hoped sincerely that she would recover some of her old combativeness. He did not think of himself as any kind of solution, knew in fact that she would once again include him among her disappointments, and that he too would recognize her as one of his. But what he had said was true: he still wanted her in his life. They would remain antagonists, but perhaps that was no bad thing, perhaps that was the mode that would keep them both functioning as they had at the beginning. And perhaps that antagonism would be their weapon against helplessness, or dependency. He had discovered, somewhat to his surprise, that in her presently reduced company he had become more of a man. That was the accomplishment he would bring home from France. Had she not been slightly impressed by his announcement that he was leaving just as she was claiming the right to leave first?

He glanced at his watch, another habit that had always irritated her. She would be gone by now and he would have to wait for a telephone call to tell him she was back. Although he would soon be gone himself it was her return that would restore the natural order. If that day came, when he himself were returned, a new man, he would betray no yearning, no anxiety, as he had done so many times in the past. They would meet again almost casually, and thus invent a new friendship. This was an ideal he knew that nothing would change. The only permitted change was the landscape, and on this point his thinking remained fixed. He would go to Paris, if only to prove himself as good as his word. It was all a question of style.

And if neither of them came back? If Sarah's impatience and his own solitude reasserted themselves, so that the old incompatibility surfaced, if, conceivably, they found a kind of contentment in new surroundings, what then? But the idea had to be tested, for stasis was not to be borne. That was the challenge they now faced, and he granted them both a certain courage in taking such a step.

He returned his books, bought a couple of shirts, and had his hair cut. 'Shan't be seeing you again,' said his usual hairdresser.

'Oh?'

'Going back to Australia.'

'Oh, I'm so sorry. Any particular reason?'

'Homesick, I guess. And I've done what I set out to do, seen Europe. I'll be quite glad to go, really. What do they say? Time to move on.'

'Yes, they do say that rather a lot. I may move on myself.'

But she was not interested, had already removed herself from the scene. Even at a young age she felt the melancholy of departure. He handed over a larger tip than usual, and received a hug in return.

'You've been great,' she said.

'Come back and see us some time. And good luck.'

They were both moved, more by the force that seemed to be directing them than by their own decisions. It was then that he knew that he must move swiftly, though still wishing that he had some reason to stay. But finally it was his flat that tilted the balance. He could always come back, he reassured himself. But even coming back to the same surroundings would be preferable to never leaving them.

27

He took a valedictory walk through the neighbourhood, making a careful note of what he would leave behind. This amounted to very little: the same actions, performed at the same time, on similar days. Memory was now porous; little survived of the past to sustain him, and what did survive was infused with regret. But this regret too was valedictory, something to be renounced, as one abandons a lost cause. It was to other agencies that he now entrusted what remained of his life. Like a man at the dawn of time he put his faith in the return of the sun, the benign and vivifying light that would eventually bring fruition. He thought back to that market in Paris, the energy of those exchanges. He would observe, but not entirely as an outsider. He would find a way to absorb some of that energy and to partake of it, so that in time it might lend a sense of purpose to whatever came next.

But in fact this was an inconclusive exercise, for habit proved stronger than he had anticipated. Habit had sustained him through times of raging disappointment no less than through dull routine. All in all he found the latter more acceptable. That, he had decided, was all over. At the hairdresser's he had been surprised to note that his hair, so long grey, was now white. He seemed to have aged, exponentially, in the last few days, as if reaching this so quixotic decision to uproot himself had in fact marked the approaching end of a life, not only his own, as it was now, but the life that had sustained him for so long.

The unavoidable fact was that there was little time left.

Sarah had felt the same, but her nature had permitted her to ignore the fact, to fashion some sort of reprieve, if only a disputatious one with a putative relative. As for himself he had no such connection. That had always been the problem. His diary, once full, was now empty. He had been to all the weddings, heard about all the children, attended several funerals, and now, it seemed, was the only survivor. Even the thought of returning to this place, which he had not yet left, seemed implausible. Yet what was the alternative? He would decline but not too rapidly: his excellent health would see him through, but he would derive no pleasure from the fact of his survival. And the default mode was to go into some sort of care, which was not even to be considered. Surely an hotel was preferable. And if the Pension Franklin proved a disappointment there were other hotels, further south, that might revive that earlier fantasy. But in fact it was the memory of that market, that commerce, as if life were a practical and pleasurable certainty, that had inspired him, had made him yearn to be part of it, to embrace it with the same vivacity that had set the fantasy in motion, had indeed brought it into existence. This was the obverse of all fears, the assurance that life was still a possession to be treasured, and that its possession was unalienably his.

He bought a couple of paperbacks, which he suspected he would not read. They were more in the nature of a token, a memento of his life in this so familiar country, which, to his surprise, he seemed to be leaving. Again he reminded himself that he could always come back, that he might even envisage a life with Sarah, if her thought processes echoed his own, which he suspected might be the case. But even so the sun might beckon, and would continue to do so. That the sun was a metaphor he did not doubt, but that merely gave it more power. And she was right, as she had always been right: to be reduced to the same arguments, the same irritations, would merely spell tedium, unwanted reminiscence, a dread knowledge of time wasted. Surely a rash decision, such as he seemed to have taken, was in every way to be preferred.

Yet the familiar streets held a promise of safety, however illusory. He could live here almost unthinkingly, free to indulge his every inclination. He was solvent, housed, not obliged to invent his life, as he would be in another setting. All that notion of making it new, as he had tried to explain his uncharacteristic impulse to Sarah, now seemed pure fantasy. Although imagination was highly desirable, reason was safer. And it was reason which now reasserted itself as potential dangers took shape, dangers multiplied by distance.

Once more in the flat he went through the motions of packing a bag, then sat down, bewildered, as if the whole adventure, still to be undertaken, were some sort of madness. The days before him were empty, and the emptiness was as much of a burden as it always had been. Yet his mind had still to be made up, and without some sort of outside agency he was doomed to remain in this divided state, apparently without any form of resolution.

When the telephone rang he sprang to answer it, thinking Sarah must have been subject to the same sort of paralysis. But it was another voice that roused him.

'Hello, hello. I'm back. Just landed. I was wondering if I could just . . .'

Quietly he replaced the receiver. Just as quietly he picked up his bag, closed the door behind him, and set out for France, beginning his journey to another life. Making it new.